Oregon at Last !

Oregon at Last!

by A. Rutgers van der Loeff

Illustrated by CHARLES GEER

Translated from the Dutch
by Roy Edwards

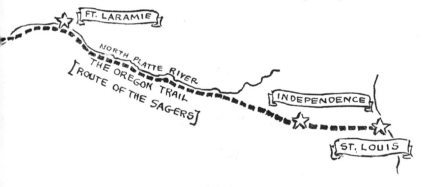

WILLIAM MORROW & COMPANY

New York, 1961

Western
Americana
PZ
7
R973
O6

English translation copyright © 1961 by
University of London Press Ltd.

First published in Dutch in the Netherlands in 1954
under the title *De Kinderkaravaan*.

English translation first published in Great Britain
in 1961 under the title *Children on the Oregon Trail*.
Published in the United States in 1962.

Printed in the United States of America.

Library of Congress Catalog Card Number 62-9866

Contents

Introduction 7

1 Covered Wagon Caravan 13

2 Indian Attack 24

3 Buffalo Stampede 43

4 "We'll Stay Together" 60

5 The Children Alone 76

6 Fight with the Bears 92

7 Quicksand 110

8 Pursued by Fire 128

9 Fort Boise 155

10 The Great Cloudburst 184

11 The Bear's Den 196

12 Oregon at Last! 210

Introduction

This story is based on historical facts.

It all happened more than a hundred years ago. North America was, for the most part, an unknown, undeveloped country. Only explorers and fur trappers had wandered through the immense forests, over the rolling prairies, and across the rugged mountains. Now it was the turn of the first pioneers—men and women with children, who looked for a new life in a new land. It was the time when Americans in the East swarmed out into the undeveloped West, in order to take possession of millions and millions of acres of new ground.

When John Sager was eight years old, his father caught the pioneering fever. The family loaded all their goods and chattels into a covered wagon, harnessed four oxen to it, and left the east coast of the United States for the Middle West.

After a whole summer of traveling, they reached

7

the Mississippi. There they settled down. Not far from the frontier town of St. Louis, Henry Sager staked out some land, cleared it, ploughed it, built a log house on it. And so they had a farm again. John hunted and fished, wandered round with an old rifle in his hand. He caught a raccoon and tamed it, learned the habits of animals and how to mimic the sounds they made. He got to know the Indians, whom he saw come on their ponies, wrapped in blankets, to trade with the white settlers. He also took part in skirmishes and learned to fight; he was not often frightened.

But he was not destined to grow up in that region, for his father was seized with the desire to go on. Henry Sager had the nature of a true pioneer; he wanted to explore, he wanted to see and reclaim new land, he wanted to join with the other pioneers in making America great. But the work of such pioneers was risky. The Indians did not look on meekly while their ancestral hunting grounds were destroyed by the white people; and nature in that wilderness of the far West was cruel, treacherous, dangerous—though fabulously beautiful. Henry Sager was drawn by that wondrous land as by a magnet. Hitherto he had not dared to give way to temptation; his family was a large one, and the journey was perilous. But the previous summer —that was to say, in 1843—a great caravan of emigrants had gone for the first time to Oregon, in the Northwest. That summer another caravan was to go; and he had the opportunity of selling his land and his farmhouse to newcomers from the East for a good price. This time he felt he could take the risk. The future of his children would lie in that splendid country yonder.

When they went, John was thirteen years and eight months old.

A. Rutgers van der Loeff

Oregon at Last !

CHAPTER 1

Covered Wagon Caravan

The River Laramie flowed wild and roaring, broad and foaming, through the green, hilly landscape; but in that dry season it was nowhere more than about three feet deep. Here and there spikes of rock stuck up in it, and the low banks were stony and rough. Willows grew along it, and thickets of cottonwood trees.

Somewhat higher up the valley, toward the foot of the first hills, lay Fort Laramie.

It was a low, oblong building, with a palisade of

wooden posts on top of the stone walls. Those outer walls formed the rear side of all the rooms in the fort, which opened onto the inner courtyard. It was a good, strong fort, in which the factor and his sixteen men could feel safe. Alone in the wilderness, six hundred and sixty-seven miles from the last outpost of the inhabited world, Fort Laramie was the principal trading point on the route to Oregon and California.

On this blazing afternoon in June, 1844, not a man was to be seen in the courtyard. Alone in the office, two clerks of the American Fur Company were hunched yawning at their high desks, sending their goose quills scratching over the paper on which they were drawing up an inventory of the fort's stock of food. A big caravan of emigrants was expected to arrive shortly, and then it would be important to know what you had in the house.

Three men sat talking together under the cool arch of the gate in the tower. One of them was Thomas Fitzpatrick, the famous guide and trapper, who knew as few others did the enormous expanse of the Rocky Mountains and the wilderness to the east and west of them. He was telling the factor, Boudeau, and the officer commanding the small detachment of government troops how he had managed to dodge groups of Sioux Indians on the warpath on his way from the Rockies to the fort.

Suddenly a little Indian on a prairie pony came storming toward the gate. He was a Dakota Indian, and he had come to say that his whole village was on its way there because the train of emigrants would arrive very soon. Scouts had given them the information. The Dakotas' chief intended to ask the emigrants to invite his people to a feast.

"Hm," muttered Fitzpatrick, "I've seen them feasts before. They're nothing but barefaced robbery. All them darned Indians are out for is to get the last few pounds of coffee and flour out of the poor, exhausted greenhorns. And if they don't get their way, worse things happen. A farmer who hits the trail for the wilderness is the craziest creature on two legs."

He went on grumbling. "They do just about every silly thing they can do. At night they leave their saddles and harness hanging up outside, and next morning all they find is rags of leather, gnawed to bits by the coyotes. They don't know how to keep their cattle together, and at night their guards nod off to sleep and leave the road wide open for Indian horse thieves. They don't know the first thing about anything! They overload their wagons, and on the rocky ground the axles break; they get drowned in cloudbursts, they get lost in sandstorms, and if there should be a tiny patch of quicksand anywhere, they get stuck in it. It's a sheer miracle any of 'em reach the other side of the mountain alive."

"Man!" shouted Boudeau, suddenly appearing beside him. "There they are!"

It was not the emigrants; it was the Indians.

Within a few minutes the hills on the other side of the river were covered with a disorderly horde of Indians, on horseback and on foot. The foremost of them had already reached the bank, and plunged into the foaming water. In the twinkling of an eye, the river was alive with dogs, horses, and human beings. Soon the entire cavalcade came swarming up the bank to the flat open space behind the fort.

In less than an hour, sixty tepees were standing there. Several hundred horses were grazing on the surrounding prairie, and dogs were running all over the place. The men approached the fort; small children shouted and screamed right under its walls.

The inhabitants of the fort had not yet recovered from the tumult when Boudeau suddenly bawled to his Indian wife to bring him his spyglass. He stood on the wall looking through it for a couple of minutes. Pointing to the east, he shouted, "By thunder, there come the emigrants!"

It was some time before they could be seen with the naked eye: four long columns of ox wagons with white covers, jostled by a sea of cattle and men on horseback—a laboriously moving caravan stubbornly forging ahead against the misty blue background of rolling hills in the east.

"There they are, them there backwoods farmers on the prairie, them poor tenderfeet in the wilderness of the West!" Fitzpatrick grumbled beside Boudeau.

An hour later, the first wagons had reached the river. Without halting or hesitating for a moment, they plunged in, heavily, awkwardly. Slowly and sluggishly the draught oxen waded through the strongly flowing water and then laboriously climbed up the opposite bank. The drivers shouted and cracked their whips; the wagons rumbled along, lurching and swaying.

The caravan made straight for the fort, until it almost reached the gate, when the wagons wheeled round in a circle and stopped. For some time all was quiet. The emigrants were preparing their camp. But no sooner had they finished doing that when the fort was, as it were, taken by storm.

A crowd of lean, sun-tanned faces under broad-brimmed hats suddenly appeared before the gate. Staring eyes—exclamations of amazement—tears, in the case of some of the women. They had covered nearly seven hundred miles through the unknown prairie wilderness, and this was the first patch of white civilization they had come across. And it would be about the last. . . .

That night a group of men sat talking in the courtyard of Fort Laramie, in the delicious cool of evening.

Without exception, their faces were serious, almost somber. The guide and the factor were telling the pioneers what the remainder of their journey would be like.

"From now on, you'll find next to no grass for your cattle, and you'll meet precious few buffalo on your way. What are you going to live on, and how do you propose to get those heavy wagons over the mountains with your oxen weakened as they are?"

"What Dr. Whitman did last year with *his* caravan, we can do too. He's blazed the trail for us.

Our wagons will follow the tracks of his; that's how we'll get there. The valleys of Oregon will be occupied by our people, and our children will be happy there."

Henry Sager spoke with such strength of conviction that the sneer even died from the lips of that hard-bitten prairie man and mountain hunter, Fitzpatrick.

But the men in whose name Sager spoke continued to look gloomy. They had been traveling for forty days now from their starting point, Independence, Missouri. They were disheartened by the rigors and disappointments of their arduous journey; the hoofs of many of the animals were so worn that they could hardly get along on them. At that rate, what was the future going to be like? For they had not yet covered half the route, and the worst part was still to come.

"Leave some of your cattle behind here. In their place, you can have packhorses and mules from us, and we'll let you have some coffee and sugar as well," Boudeau suggested.

Coffee and sugar! If anyone had told them three months before that they would one day barter their precious cattle for coffee and sugar, they would have given him a rough answer. But now . . .

coffee and sugar had a wondrous attraction. And the feast the Dakotas were extorting from them was disheartening too. They would need extra supplies for that, anyway. But they dared not refuse to offer it.

"If I was you," said the factor, "I'd push on ahead as fast as you can. You've still got a long way to go, and you want to reach your destination before winter sets in. As far as Fort Hall, the journey'll be comfortable enough. But take my advice—leave some of your cattle behind, buy some horses instead. Convert some of your heavy wagons into two-wheeled carts, so that you'll be able to get along more quickly and more lightly."

"We'll think about it," said Henry Sager pensively.

The following night the feast for the Indians took place.

The women, although they were tired out, had had to bake cakes and bread, and their eyes smarted from the smoke of the fires. The men sat calculating how much tobacco they would have to give up. But the children nearly went off their heads with joy. It had been so long since they had

had any celebrations, and there had been such delicious smells in the air all day.

Round the Sager family's wagon was a tremendous stir and bustle. All the children had had to put red flannel shirts on. Mother Sager and Louise, the oldest girl, had already washed the dirty ones; they hung flapping from clotheslines between the cottonwood trees.

John buckled his belt of snakeskin tight, and felt for the hunting knife at his hip. Yes . . . there it was; you never knew what might happen. With his sturdy shoulders John looked more like fifteen than thirteen. Francis, who was eleven years old, dark and slightly built, followed him everywhere. Louise had washed and combed her long, light-brown hair, and was now running around with a couple of soaking wet plaits, looking for Lizzy. Lizzy had to be washed and combed too, but she had seen the water and had fled as far as her fat, unsteady little legs would carry her. Catherine was supposed to be helping to look for her, but she didn't want to. She sat pulling at her short, dark-red curls, through which it was impossible to get a comb. Louise was in charge of things at the wagon, for Mother was on duty at one of the three big fires where the coffee was being made.

John had offered to go and work at the fire in
his mother's place. He had seen how unwell his
mother felt; she had been deathly pale these last
few days, and this morning she had been so dizzy
when she lifted the bacon tub in the wagon that
she had almost fallen down. Nevertheless, she had
refused to accept John's offer.

"I'd sooner you helped Louise with the babies,"
she had said.

John strolled round the wagon and his family
like a sheep dog round his sheep. Francis sat down
in the grass, chewed a bit of stick, and contented
himself with following John with his eyes.

Suddenly they heard a noise. The Indians were
coming! With faces full of expectation, they came
into the camp: old men with gray hair, warriors in
peace costume, youths, women and children, color-
fully dressed. They all sat down, wrapped in their
blankets, in a semicircle, with the chief in the middle and his warriors on either side of him. Then
came the braves and the youths, and finally the
squaws with the children. Coffee and cake were
put in front of them. Before the emigrants knew
where it had gone to, everything had disappeared,

to the accompaniment of loud shouts and vehement gestures of satisfaction.

The Indians feasted, danced, shouted, and sang. The whites looked on. The sun went down. Dark clouds hung above the hills.

There, where the sun had sunk behind that black band of clouds—there was the West, there lay their future, there they would go, despite all difficulties. This meeting with the Dakotas, who had journeyed for a week to collect a cup of coffee and a slice of cake, had gone off peacefully at any rate.

Three days later, the emigrants went on their way.

They had had a bit of a rest. Seven of the sixty-nine wagons had been converted into two-wheeled carts. Some of the cattle remained behind; and in their place, Boudeau had supplied thirty-five pack horses and sixteen mules with packsaddles, and some coffee and sugar.

CHAPTER 2

Indian Attack

From Fort Laramie, which lay in the fork between the Laramie and North Platte rivers, the caravan followed the bow-shaped course of the North Platte.

Often, however, they were several miles away from it. It was difficult to find the best terrain for the wagons; the hills were steep, and the ground was littered with enormous boulders. The guide, who rode in front, kept his men busy galloping to and fro to search out the most suitable route. They

went higher and higher. Before them lay the tremendous peaks and ridges of the Rocky Mountains.

Toward nightfall they generally managed to find
a perfectly satisfactory camping place, with good
grass for the animals, running water, and wood for
the fires. Day's journeys of seventeen and eighteen
miles were nothing out of the ordinary. That was
fine.

No mishaps occurred since one accident, immediately after they had left Fort Laramie, in which
the Ford family's wagon had been so badly damaged that it was only fit for the scrap heap. The
Fords and their belongings had been distributed
among other wagons, and Mrs. Ford had joined
the Sagers in their wagon, because Mrs. Sager was
expecting a baby any day.

The farther and higher they went, the less grass
grew; the landscape looked nothing like that splendid, blossoming, rolling prairie of the first weeks
of their journey. Nor did it resemble the hard, dry
buffalo plains which they had subsequently taken
weeks to cross. There was more timber now,
though, and hence they no longer had to depend
chiefly on dried buffalo droppings for fuel for their
fires.

Over and over again, it was necessary to cross some wide, muddy creek flowing from the River Platte. But there were always places which could be easily forded. However, it was a more difficult matter to cross the broad, swiftly flowing river itself, as they had to do early one morning.

The water there was higher than it had been in the Laramie. The guide and his men repeatedly galloped their horses into the stream, while the front of the caravan stood waiting on the bank; but there was no ford to be found. They would have to swim for it. Someone would have to take over to the other side the line along which the wagons would be able to cross the river like ferryboats. It was a dangerous job, because treacherous whirlpools eddied and boiled in the middle of the broad stream. There came a blast on the bugle: volunteers forward!

John Sager was sitting on the bank. He was biting with clenched teeth the stem of an empty pipe of his father's, which he had upside down in his mouth. If only he were older! He knew for certain that they would not give him a chance.

Nobody came forward. But John's face cleared when he suddenly saw his father advancing to the front; his father was riding a good horse which was quite capable of holding its own against the current.

But voices of protest went up. A couple of older men walked toward Henry Sager. As father of a family, they did not want him to run such a risk.

Then a little black mustang came galloping up from the rear of the caravan. Its rider, a young man named Walton, seized the rope from the hands of Sager, and drove his horse into the river.

The point on the other bank directly opposite the wagon train did not seem to be a bad landing place. But Walton went into the water at an angle against the current, for in the middle the river would no doubt drive him and his horse downstream.

The horse was swimming now, its head bobbing regularly up and down. The man was swimming beside it.

What a long time it took! John sat looking on in acute suspense. But his father called to him. He had to come and help. The men had begun to prepare the vehicles for crossing. The oxen were being unyoked.

Suddenly a shout of joy went up from a little group of women and children who were standing on the bank. Man and horse had reached the other side. Walton was now busy making the line fast. He signaled that the crossing could begin.

The wagons were coupled to each other, and one by one they rumbled along the rope into the water, after which, like so many floating arks, with women, children, and household bits and pieces aboard, they began to slide across to the other side.

Now it was the turn of the cattle. The first oxen went into the water upstream from the wagons. At the head went five men, each on the downstream side of one ox. They held one hand against its withers and swam with the other, prodding and urging the ungainly animal to keep to a straight line, in spite of the powerful current. Men on horseback were driving the other cattle into the water; cows, oxen, mules, and horses with riders were swimming across the broad river in six or seven rows beside each other.

John had asked his father whether he might be allowed to go with their cattle.

"Father—I can do it! Really I can! And this horse is a very good swimmer."

His father glanced at him thoughtfully. Then he said, "Right, lad."

John saw his mother's pallid face in the shade of the gray-white cover of their wagon. Her dark eyes were full of worry, but she said nothing. Francis, sitting beside her, looked at him admiringly.

The horse swam splendidly. John felt almost uncomfortably safe on her back. It was like crossing the river on a sofa. The oxen swam well too. Only Charley seemed uneasy. John even had trouble getting him into the water. When they were nearly halfway across, the animal began to drift downstream, in the direction of the wagons. John spurred his horse, and she was soon swimming beside the ox.

Charley became even more restive.

John took a quick decision; he slid from the saddle, and the horse went on, swimming more swiftly without him. He reached out for the ox's head, but before he realized what was happening, a whirlpool sucked both of them down.

After a terrible moment of black suffocation, he rose to the surface again; he gasped for breath, but all he got was a mouthful of water. He was choking, his lungs seemed on the point of cracking, there was a bursting pain in his chest. He swam with wild strokes, blindly, until he felt himself seized by another whirlpool, which again sucked him deep down below the surface.

He was going to drown, and he would never see

them again, not Francis, or Cathie, or Lizzy or anyone else . . . anyone. Suddenly he felt something heavy bump against him down in the water. His hand groped for support there—it was the hairy shank of his ox; he rose to the surface along the animal's side, discovering that it was now swimming at an angle against the current, evidently trying to rejoin the herd.

John remained swimming beside its head, occasionally glancing gratefully at the mild, frightened eyes of the beast. He had wanted to rescue Charley, and it was Charley who had rescued him.

On the other bank, the horse was waiting patiently for him. She had got almost dry already, in the sun. She was nibbling at a big tuft of grass in the shade of a red willow. John hardly glanced up or around. He threw himself down in the grass, then he shut his eyes. An hour later his father found him there, fast asleep.

The great trek went on.

That day began like any other.

At four o'clock in the morning, when the rising sun stood like a red ball above the gray landscape, the guards fired off their rifles, as a sign that the hours of sleep were past. Women, men, and children streamed out of every tent and wagon. The gently smouldering fires from the previous night were replenished with wood, and bluish-gray clouds of smoke began to float through the morning air. Bacon was fried; coffee was made by those who still had some.

All this took place within the corral, the ring which had been made by driving the wagons into a circle and fastening them firmly to each other by means of the shafts and chains. This formed a strong barricade through which even the most vicious ox could not break, and in the event of an attack by the Sioux Indians it would be a bulwark not to be despised.

Outside the corral the cattle and horses cropped the sparse grass in a wide circle.

At five o'clock sixty men mounted their horses and rode out of the camp. They fanned out through the crowds of cattle until they reached the outskirts of the herd; once there, they encircled it and began to drive all the cattle before them. The animals moved slowly in the direction of the camp. There the drivers picked their teams of oxen out from the densely herded mass and led them into the corral, where the yoke was put upon them.

From six o'clock until seven, the camp was extra-busy; breakfast was eaten, tents were struck, wagons were loaded, and the teams of draught oxen and mules were made ready to be harnessed to their wagons and carts. Everyone knew that whoever was not ready when the signal to start was blown at seven o'clock would be doomed for that day to travel in the dusty rear of the caravan.

There were sixty-eight wagons. They were divided into seventeen columns, each consisting of four wagons. Each column took it in turn to lead the way. The section that was at the head today would bring up the rear tomorrow, unless a driver had missed his place in the row through laziness or negligence, and had to travel behind by way of punishment.

It was ten minutes to seven.

There were gaps everywhere in the corral; the teams of oxen were being harnessed in front of the wagons, the chains clanked. The women and children had taken their places under the canvas covers. The guide was standing among his assistants at the head of the line, ready to mount his horse and show the way.

As soon as the herdsmen were ready, they hurried to the rear of their herd, in order to drive them together and get them ready for today's march.

Seven o'clock.

An end had come to the busy running and walking to and fro, the cracking of whips, the shouts of command to the oxen, and the bawling from wagon to wagon. Every driver was at his post. A bugle rang out! The guide and his escort mounted their horses, the four wagons of the leading section rumbled out of the camp and formed the first column, the rest took their places with the regularity of clockwork, and the caravan slowly moved forward over the broad plateau, far above the foaming river.

A new hard day had begun. It was particularly hard for the Sagers, who were having to do without the help of Mrs. Ford, since she, had gone to look after a sick child.

The sun rose high in the sky. It was hot and stuffy under the canvas tilts, which were thick with dust. Toward noon the children everywhere began to bicker and whimper. But in the Sager family's wagon, they had other things to worry about.

John, who had been riding for hours in the blazing sun, beside the heads of the foremost yoke of oxen, was given an order by his father, who was sitting on the driver's bench in the front of the wagon.

Immediately he galloped forward. He had to fetch the doctor.

The doctor was a veterinary surgeon; the emigrants did not have a real doctor with them. But the vet had already helped the people considerably, as well as the animals.

John rode with all his might. Why on earth didn't the doctor travel in the middle of the caravan? From his father's face the boy had seen that the matter was urgent.

Meanwhile, Henry Sager had driven his wagon out of the line. He stopped. "All the children must get out," he ordered. "Go and collect buffalo droppings and make a fire. Louise has to boil as much water as she can."

Before Louise left the wagon, she filled the big kettle with water, scooping it up in a little tin bowl from the barrel in the back of the wagon. She cast a timid glance at her mother, who lay still and white on the tarpaulin. Mother caught Louise's eye and gave her a gentle, encouraging nod. If only that doctor would come quickly!

The doctor came.

With his long legs, he stepped from the saddle into the wagon in one stride. Then he wiped the sweat and dust out of his eyes with the back of his hand.

To the children, it seemed to take a long time. The water had already been boiling for quite a while. No one had asked for it yet, and they did not dare look into the wagon.

In the distance ahead of them hung a thick cloud of dust, behind which the caravan was hidden. They would fall very far to the rear. John knew that that was dangerous—stragglers ran the risk of being attacked; but he said nothing. Now and again his father came out and glanced around, scanned the trail behind them. But the horizon was clear and empty.

Until John suddenly perceived a tiny cloud of dust.

He started. He knew that that could only mean that Indians were approaching.

"Father!" he shouted.

Henry Sager stuck his head out of the wagon.

John pointed to the east, where the cloud of dust above their own tracks had now grown rather larger.

Father Sager went back into the wagon with the kettle of boiling water, but came out again a moment later with five rifles and two pistols. John had already pulled his own pistol from its holster. His father gave him a rifle.

"All the children except John and Louise, get under the wagon," he commanded quietly. But it was easy to see that that calmness required all the self-control he had. His strong neck was fiery red, and the veins on his forehead were thick and purple.

"Take these," he said to his eldest daughter, and Louise stood with three rifles in her arms, staring at the approaching cloud of dust as if turned to stone.

Father put the powder horn, lead, and ramrods down beside her.

John was still on his horse and had laid his rifle across the saddlebow in front of him, as he had always seen the trappers do.

But his father said, "Are you mad, boy? Get down and tie the horse up in front, along with the oxen. Do you want to serve as a target, and be shot from the saddle?"

Francis pushed the smaller children under the wagon. Catherine began to resist, crying and kicking. "Stop howling, you little idiot," Francis snapped nervously, trying to make his voice sound as manly as possible. Matilda and Lizzy thought it rather a nice game; as a rule, they were never allowed to go under the wagon.

Father Sager climbed back in again. He brought out two empty water casks, and the only bag of flour they had left. He stood the two casks upright beside the wagon, near one of the rear wheels, and laid the sack of flour across them.

"Come to the back here," he ordered John and Louise. "And remember—don't stir from cover. We fire along to one side of this, and between the casks. Louise, you load the rifles when we've fired them." To John he said nothing, he only looked at him.

A sound came from the wagon. It was the crying of a tiny baby.

Father Sager gritted his teeth, and behaved as if he had not heard anything. The sound came again, more distinctly this time. Then he looked at his two eldest children; he almost had tears in his eyes.

"May God help us to protect that young life," he said. "It's not certain that the Indians mean mischief. And our rifles are good sound ones. John, don't fire too soon; let 'em come close."

They waited in suspense. It was now easy to see that the cause of the cloud was horsemen—not

many, perhaps half a dozen, Indians on prairie
ponies. They were superior in numbers, but they
could not take cover anywhere. There was no
brushwood in which they could conceal themselves.

"May God help us to protect that young life,"
Father had said. Those words made an indelible
impression on John.

There, inside the wagon, a new brother or sister
was lying—a new life, and it was theirs. Just imagine, suppose something should happen to it!

The Indians were so close now that John could
see that one of them was carrying a rifle; the others
had bows and arrows.

There . . . the first arrow came whizzing through
the air. Its iron tip bored through the canvas cover
of the wagon; the feathered tail stood buzzing and
quivering. A shot rang out, but Father motioned
to John to wait.

Then . . . they both fired at the same time.

The foremost Indian, the one with the rifle, fell
sideways from his horse, wounded. The animal
dragged him a short distance along the ground.
The other members of the troop swerved away
immediately, rode round in a great circle at tremendous speed, and charged again.

Once more Henry and John Sager fired their two rifles, while the arrows whistled above their heads.

The second Indian was shot out of the saddle. One of his comrades seized him just in time, and pulled him onto his horse, in front of him.

John's hat was whipped from his head; a dry tap sounded; he glanced around. An arrow had drilled its way deep into the woodwork of the wagon, carrying hat and all. Then he heard a splash—he just glimpsed the arms of the doctor, who had emptied a bowl of water out through the tilt.

Louise pushed another freshly loaded rifle into John's hands. But it was no longer necessary. The Indians had now picked up the two wounded men, and were galloping off in a wide arc. The two riderless ponies were running far away in the distance. Soon there was nothing to be seen but slowly settling dust.

"Indian cattle thieves," said Father Sager brusquely. "They'll have been disappointed."

He took the sack of flour and climbed into the wagon with it. An arrow had pierced it; a white trail of its precious contents was trickling down through a little hole.

A moment later he stuck his head outside again. "You can all come in," he said solemnly.

One by one they climbed into the wagon, John leading the way. He tried to behave very sedately, but inwardly he was trembling. Louise had John's hat in her hands, and was trying to smooth out the dents in it. Stretching out his long arms, Henry Sager lifted Matilda and Lizzy from the ground.

There lay Mother, her pale face with those big eyes laughing sweetly up at them, and her long dark hair spread out on both sides of her head against the white canvas. The doctor threw away a last bowl of water, dried his hands, and gave Father Sager a hearty slap on the back. Only then did the children see that Father was holding something in his arms. It was a baby, washed and combed, with a big forelock of black hair, looking ridiculously tiny in Mother's purple silk shawl.

"She'll weigh about nine pounds, I guess—an enormous child!" said the doctor.

An enormous child!

John glanced at Louise, but Louise was gazing, fascinated, at the baby. Then he looked at Francis, who looked back at him with a grin. An *enormous* child! It was really laughable. But the baby was a girl—that was nice. A new little sister, a very small sister. Perhaps it was because they had just escaped from great danger, while the baby was being born, or because, after that fight, John felt more of a man than ever; but in any case he had a burning desire to take his little sister in his arms, and protect her against everything forever.

But Father put the baby down again beside its mother.

They went on their knees in a circle round mother and child. The doctor and Father took their hats off; John tore his from Louise's hands, and held the damaged hat over his chest, just like Father, and closed his eyes. His father prayed aloud in a firm, deep voice.

"O Lord, we commend this child to your care. Her name shall be Indepentia. And she shall be baptized in the new land, in the valley of the River Columbia in Oregon. Amen."

Late in the evening, the Sager family's wagon rolled into the camp at Willow Creek Spring. The sun had already set. Boys and girls were sitting on the sandy bank of the creek, dangling their warm feet in the cool water. The splashing they made mingled with their soft, laughing voices. Somewhere a violin was being played.

Outside the guide's tent, the leaders of the wagon train were sitting in council in the light of the fire. Henry Sager walked up to them and said something. Heavily they got to their feet; one by one they shook his hand. Their faces were set in serious expressions under their broad-brimmed hats. Indepentia Sager was the first covered-wagon baby of their caravan.

"The best of luck go with her," was their wish.

CHAPTER 3

Buffalo Stampede

The caravan went on.

Accidents happened to the wagons every day. In that rough country the axles gave way over and over again, poles broke, hoops came off the wheels. The columns and the individual vehicles became more and more scattered. Only too often stray groups of wagons did not come rolling into the camping place until late in the evening, sometimes deep in the night.

The men and women had a hard time of it. But

they remained brave and tenacious; after all, they *were* getting on, every day brought them closer to the promised land, for on the average they were still covering twelve to fifteen miles a day.

They traveled south, round Independence Rock, one of the most remarkable sights on their route.

It was solitary, a completely bare mountain of gray granite, towering up from an open plain; at its foot, along its southern side, flowed the lovely Sweetwater River, bordered by an exquisite strip of green grass, which was twenty to thirty feet wide, so that the wagons could easily make their way along it, in one single column. The clear water of the river actually tasted sweetish, and was a real treat for the emigrants.

In its gray nakedness, the Rock was most impressive. The names of trappers and explorers had been cut in it, together with the dates.

Henry Sager took his sons to look at it. He made them dismount and, hat in hand, read the inscriptions left by those courageous men who had defied the great dangers of that land in order to chart the way for those who should come after them.

"This rock has been called the Great Register of the Desert," said Henry Sager. "Look . . . here it says: 'The Oregon Company arrived July 26,

1843.' That was last year; and they were the first caravan of pioneers ever to pass through this country. It's a pity Dr. Whitman didn't add his own name."

"Why?" asked Francis.

"Who's Dr. Whitman?" asked John.

With a strange glow in his eyes, Henry Sager gazed fixedly toward the west, as he answered, almost absently:

"Marcus Whitman is a medical missionary who works among the Indians at Waiilatpu, in the Columbia Valley. He fights for his dream that one day Oregon will become American territory! The British of the Hudson's Bay Company are blocking our way there. They would like it to become British. The Indian tribes, who live from hunting, probably curse both of us. But Whitman foresees that it would be possible for thousands and thousands of Americans to carve out a happy life for themselves in the fertile valleys of Oregon. And that's why, a year ago, by superhuman exertions, he blazed a trail here for the first emigrants. God grant his work will not have been in vain!"

"Is he going to baptize Indepentia?" asked John, sticking closer to homely facts.

"Yes . . . when we reach his mission post, we'll

ask him to christen our Indepentia," said Henry Sager.

With obvious effort, he tore himself away from his vision, and returned to concrete reality. "We've got to get back to Mother, lads!"

That day they made good progress, and before sundown they pitched their camp within sight of the Devil's Gate. In the evening, buffalo yarns were told round the campfire. There was to be a buffalo hunt the next day, but John would not be allowed to go. It was considered too dangerous. Anyone who aspired to go buffalo hunting had to sit extremely firmly in the saddle and be sure of his aim, for otherwise the man would go down instead of the buffalo.

The pioneers had had some experience of that at the start of their journey, long before they reached Fort Laramie.

In the beginning, the first faint shapes of buffalo on a distant ridge had been the signal for a general exodus of everyone who could sit in a saddle and fire a gun. But they had soon found that unpracticed hunters on unpracticed horses achieved nothing. The horses became jumpy. Once in the vicinity of a herd of buffalo, with their rank scent, they began to rear with trembling nostrils, to twist and turn and snort; and, despite a vigorous use of spurs by their riders, they kept a respectful distance from the quarry. And when the herd got irritated and came charging forward, the situation was deadly dangerous. A bull buffalo was a terrible adversary. As a rule, the horse was more sensible than its reckless rider, and even a wounded buffalo was often enough to make it gallop back to camp, in spite of all that bridle and spurs could do. Only by repeated practice with an experienced hunter was it possible to train a horse for buffalo hunting.

The weather had remained good ever since they had left Fort Laramie. In fact, it was almost too good to be true. But that night, the wind came up.

At first it was not frightening, but nevertheless the sensible ones among the emigrants went out to tie down their tents and wagon covers extra tight.

The wind grew stronger; soon it had become a raging storm. Everything squeaked, creaked, groaned, and clattered. The animals outside the corral stood huddled against each other in dense droves, snorting, restless, lowing from hundreds of throats. Dogs yelped, children cried in the wagons, which shuddered on their wheels. With a tremendous creaking and cracking, the only tall tree in the camping ground crashed to the ground.

The families of the emigrants crouched together in their wagons or tents, hands over their ears, eyes big with terror.

Then it began to thunder. And it was as if the rolling claps of thunder and the blinding sheets of lightning fanned the storm. In many wagons, people began to pray.

Deafeningly, the tempest raged over the camp. Vehicles were beaten to matchwood, tarpaulins tore loose, tents blew down. Then it began to pour in torrents.

The people of the caravan had never experienced such weather in their lives. Never had they seen such persistent, vivid lightning, never had they heard such a continuous, terrifying rumble of thunder, never had they had to endure such impenetrable sheets of rain. The jets of rain made a somber, rushing sound, and spouted holes in the ground. It was as if the world was to come to an end that night; the whole universe trembled and shook. At one moment the immediate vicinity, with beaten-down brushwood and wrecked wagons, was lit up in a blinding white glare by the lightning, and at the next moment everyone and everything had been shut in by a wall of utter darkness.

Toward sunrise the thunderstorm ceased as suddenly as it had begun. But its cessation hardly brought relief. The destruction was too terrible to be described. Half the wagons had been badly damaged, and some were completely beyond repair. The Sager family's wagon had come off comparatively well. Father Sager and John had gone out in good time and done everything they could to make secure what could be secured. And their wagon was a strong, well-built one.

Cathie and Lizzy, who had howled all night without stopping, were sleeping like logs now; Matilda was lying quietly beside them on the blanket, looking up with open eyes at the gray-white canvas of the tilt, which was slowly drying in the warmth of the first rays of the sun. For all her five years she had been braver than nine-year-old Cathie, and less worried than twelve-year-old Louise, who had listened to the tumult outside with wide eyes in a face drawn with fright and white as chalk.

Father Sager left his family behind in the care of Mother and John. He had to go and confer with other responsible men of the expedition, to decide what had to be done. It was obvious that more than half the wagon train would not be able to start that day.

After a conference lasting more than an hour, it was decided that the caravan should split into two. The quicker wagons and teams had long been held up and kept back by those which could only go more slowly. Everything that could travel would push on immediately, while the rest would remain behind to carry out the necessary repairs and to recover a little from the ordeal of the night. They were only a few days' journey from Fort Bridger, a recently established, extremely primitive outpost, where Jim Bridger, an old guide and trapper, had fitted up a simple smithy and carpenter's shop to serve the emigrant trains en route. Perhaps the two parties would meet again there; and perhaps not. In any case, they would cover the rest of the journey independently of each other.

Henry Sager remained with the rear group. Not because he would not have been able to travel with the fast party, but because no other man so able as a leader declared himself willing to stay behind. Moreover, his wife had never recovered her strength; she was still languid and weak; she was suffering from dysentery, which grew worse rather than better, and he himself felt less well than he cared to admit. It would be good for them to take things a bit easily. And his animals would also benefit if he granted them one or two days' more rest.

John was disappointed when he heard of the plan. He would have liked to go with the first party. But he could take such disappointments. Father had early impressed on him that he must not let circumstances get him down. And John had been a good pupil. He had as hard a head and as great a capacity for perseverance as his father. But he always resigned himself to decisions whose reasonableness he realized.

Two days later they set out again. They left the Devil's Gate on their right, and turned southwest. The weather was as fine and bright as it had been for all those weeks before the storm. But no one would ever forget the experience of that night.

John's father, on horseback, led the caravan along in the tracks of the party which had gone on in front two days before. John sat on the driver's seat. He did not like riding in the wagon, but he was glad he was at the head of the train. There they were not troubled by dust.

Louise did all the housework and looked after the little ones, for Mother lay helpless in the back of the wagon. She was so ill that she could hardly speak a word, and only smiled faintly when Louise or John laid the tiny baby down beside her to be fed.

On the second day of their journey, as the two parallel columns were rolling across the plain at the normal steady, sluggish speed of ox wagons, the drivers and outriders were startled by a strange dull noise from the north. It sounded like the rumble of a very distant storm, but the sky was as clear as could be, in the north and everywhere else.

The rumbling swelled, slowly but steadily; it grew ever louder and more ominous.

Henry Sager reined in his horse, and scanned through his spyglass the circle of hazy blue mountains bordering the green valley. Behind him, the entire caravan came to a halt.

"Stampeding buffalo," Henry Sager said curtly to the riders beside him.

He passed the spyglass across to one of them. There was a worried look on his face.

"They're coming this way at a tremendous pace. With the glass you can already see the front of the herd—yes, that enormous dark-brown mass.

They're charging down on us like a tornado. If they go over us, we might just as well be buried under a stream of lava. We've got to get out of their way."

He turned in the saddle, and shouted an order behind him. "Get moving—for all you're worth!" And he sent horsemen to the rear, on both sides of the column, to make sure his order was carried out.

John and the other drivers lashed the oxen with their whips. Voices shouted, whips cracked and swished, the cattle galloped wildly, hunted forward by the bawling herdsmen; the wagons creaked horribly now that they were being driven at such speed over the uneven ground. The last wagons had to be past the danger point before the buffalo reached it.

In no time, the caravan was one cloud of dust; no driver could see beyond the wall of dust enclosing him and his oxen. Everyone breathed dust. Everyone bit dust. The animals ran blindly behind each other, led by smell and sound.

But even the din made by the caravan was drowned by that tremendous thundering, coming nearer and nearer.

"We shan't make it," one of the foremost horsemen panted.

Henry Sager, who had been mute since giving that last order, looked at him darkly.

"*We* shall, but the last ones won't. Get to the back, and collect all the mounted men on the north side of our tail. Have all the cattle driven to the south side, behind the wagons. I'll follow you in a minute. We've got to keep going like this for a while."

The man turned his horse about and galloped off. Father Sager looked behind him. He tried to pierce the eddying clouds of dust with his eyes, but he could only hear the snorting and the thundering hoofs of the oxen behind him.

Once again, Henry Sager estimated the distance still separating them from the approaching horde of buffalo. It was high time for the last desperate measures.

He turned his horse, drove his spurs into its sides and, bending down over its neck, clenched his teeth and rode straight into the cloud of dust. In the rear he found forty or so mounted men, who were riding on the north side of the caravan, between the wagons and the threatening danger.

"Dismount!" Sager roared. "Set light to the grass and all the bushes you can find! Look alive!"

In less than no time a wall of flames blazed up.

The men withdrew behind and to either side of it.

The buffalo were close now; the dull rumble of thousands upon thousands of trampling hoofs mingled with the bellowing of thousands of throats. The ground trembled and shook with their wild galloping. They were running against the wind. The stinging smoke blew towards them. They saw the flames. But like mad creatures they still charged straight ahead. The leaders were driven forward by all that ran behind.

It seemed as if the earth would burst asunder from those thundering hoofs. Men shouted, horses tore violently at their bridles and whinnied with terror. The hairy humps of the buffalo could now be seen, and in their shaggy heads the smouldering points of their eyes, which caught the sun.

Henry Sager sat as if turned to stone. He knew his own family was safe; but these last wagons, with their precious cargo of human lives, had also been entrusted to his care.

And now he gave his last command.

"Shoot! Shoot off all the rifles and pistols, right through the flames, and here at the northern point of the fire. They've got to wheel southeast!"

Shouting, the men passed his order on. For a moment, all other sounds seemed drowned in one ear-splitting report. Gun after gun was shot off at random.

It was now or never. If fire, smoke, and shooting, all together, were of no avail, they were lost. The suspense was well-nigh unbearable. No one breathed.

But it worked!

The foremost buffalo could not stop—the force behind them was too tremendous; if they had tried to stop, they would have been trampled underfoot and pulverized. But they did begin to turn. They swung off to the left, to the southeast. Just where the wall of fire and smoke covered the tail end of the rearguard, the extreme right flank of the herd rolled by. The air throbbed with the bellowing, but the danger was past. The animals streamed by as if crazed, blind and deaf, wild and terrible because of their sheer mass; but they no longer inspired fear. With hoarse throats the men shouted a hurrah. Tears were running down the cheeks of some of them.

The train came to a standstill. The oxen were dead beat. From all the wagons, men, women, and children poured out to see the spectacle. A dozen buffalo lay dead and partly crushed beside the onward-flowing, dark-brown, hairy mass. In a sea of backs the herd rolled on; in thousands upon thousands it rolled on.

John came riding up slowly, his eyes staring fixedly at the incredible sight. He had Francis sitting behind, and little Matilda was on the saddle in front of him. Like all the others, he was gray with dust, and the sweat was running in streams down his temples.

His face, striped with dirt, broke into a smile, when Matilda turned her little head, looked up at him, and said, "It was a lot of buffalo, wasn't it, John?"

It was decided that the emigrants would go no farther that day. An hour later, while the buffalo were still streaming past, the wagons were driven into a circle. The corral was formed. The oxen were watered at a creek, and there was grass to spare for them to the west of the buffalo stampede.

At last, when the sun's beams were slanting from the west, and the bushes were casting long shadows, the stream began to come to an end. And within quite a short time not a single buffalo was to be seen with the naked eye. The wind blew the rank stench of their trail away from the camp. Where the wild horde had passed, the plain, once so green, had been churned up until it was completely black. The fire had died out on the edge of that desert.

That night, two things happened in the Sager family.

When the last red light of the sun lit up the tops of the western hills, Louise Sager sought in vain for little Matilda, who had to go to bed. It was John who finally found her and carried her to the corral and put her in their wagon.

He arrived just in time to see his father clutch at his stomach, retch, and sink to his knees with a face as white as chalk.

With the help of a neighbor, Louise and John laid him beside Mother in the wagon. Mother was feeding Indepentia. John looked tenderly at the little black head against Mother's white shoulder in the dusk of the canvas tilt. He felt quite particularly fond of that little sister of his.

Beads of sweat broke out on Father's forehead. "Now *you'll* have to look after the family, John," he said hoarsely; and those words sent a shiver down John's spine.

Surely, Father was only a bit unwell? He only meant that John would have to care for the family as long as the illness lasted.

The boy nodded reassuringly.

"And Francis is here, too, Father," he said.

Francis, who was lying in his blanket, blushed red with pleasure at John's words.

CHAPTER 4

"We'll Stay Together"

In the evening of a hot day early in July Kit Carson, one of the most famous trappers of the time, came across a small emigrants' camp between Fort Bridger and the Sublette Cutoff. Only one wagon was standing there; two horses and a number of cows were trying to find food between the stones and sagebrush.

Carson rode up at a gallop, leapt from his horse, and ordered a boy who came toward him to put out the fire.

It was a lad with hair bleached almost white by the sun and a face full of freckles. He was wearing a long red flannel shirt that came down to his knees. In his leather belt he had stuck two knives and a powder horn. The belt sagged crookedly round his narrow hips with the weight of a heavy pistol in a holster. His eyes were bright and intelligent.

Without hesitation he did as Carson told him.

He ran to the wagon, brought out a spade, and threw earth over the fire of buffalo droppings. Not until he had finished did he look up and ask, "Why do I have to do this?"

The strange man looked at him. Then he turned his eyes to the row of children's faces staring from the wagon. It was late, and they ought really to have been asleep. The big boy glanced round at them and frowned. Then he said, awkwardly pointing, "That's my brother and sisters."

"Oh, is that so?" said Carson, with a sick feeling in his stomach.

Those children were in danger. Indians were usually above killing children, but the grownups who must surely also be there ran every risk of being butchered. And if that happened, what would become of the kids? And how in the world did this one wagon come to be standing there, all on its own, in the middle of the wilderness?

"Why did I have to put out the fire?" John Sager asked again.

"Because there's a party of Sioux Indians on the warpath. They mustn't spy that smoke," Carson replied. It was best to tell the truth. "Where's your father?"

"Father and Mother are both lying ill in the wagon."

"How do you come to be alone here like this?" asked the trapper.

"The other wagons are two days' journey in front of us," the boy answered. "We couldn't get any farther. I had to repair one of the wagon axles first. But it's all right now. Father told me what to do."

"Just take me inside there, will you? I'd like to see your father," said Carson.

They walked up to the wagon. The children's faces in the white frame of the cover receded. With one foot already in the wagon, Carson turned toward the boy. "What's your name?" he asked.

"Sager," said John. "Father's name is Henry, and I am John Sager."

"Hm," said the trapper, but what he thought was, Mighty fine lad, that.

It was dark in the wagon. Carson felt and heard children's bodies creeping and squirming round him; and he heard the sound of breath being drawn in gasps somewhere at the back. He took his tinderbox out of his pocket and struck a light.

"I'm never allowed to do that in the wagon now Father's ill," said John. "Risk of fire," he added dryly.

Carson blew the flame out. He smiled to himself in the dark.

"Your eyes'll get used to the darkness," the boy's voice went on. "Father's lying in the back. Please don't tread on Indepentia's basket, that's on the left."

"Indepentia?" growled Carson.

"Our baby," John explained, with a note of pride in his voice.

Heavens above, a baby in this company, too!

His eyes did adjust themselves to the darkness. It was not long before he could make out two figures lying stretched out on a drab tarpaulin.

"That's Father and Mother," John whispered. "They sleep a lot. And Father's delirious sometimes."

Carson bent down and scrutinized the wasted white faces of the man and woman as well as he could.

"What have you got in the way of food?" he asked John in a whisper.

"The day before yesterday I shot an antelope and three rabbits, and we're still living on them. But Father and Mother can't keep any meat down. They drink water. But our water's nearly gone, and we're nowhere near any spring or river here. It's not such a good camping place," he ended shamefacedly.

Carson shook the man's shoulder. But he did not wake up. His eyes flickered half open for a moment, then closed again.

"Come outside," Carson ordered John suddenly, under his breath. He found it difficult to breathe there.

He could not help them. He had to go on. The trappers' camp at Green River Rendezvous had to be warned that the Sioux were on their way with anything but friendly intentions. He could not stay with the children even for that one night. But the lad beside him appeared to be very much of a man. If he could only see to it that they left this place at once and caught up with the others. . . .

"Listen, John," he said, laying a hand on the boy's shoulder. He noticed how muscular that shoulder and arm were. "You harness your oxen to your wagon, and drive as fast as you can, day and night, without stopping, until you come up with the rest of the troop. Do you understand? Day and night, without stopping. If you're right about them being two days' journey ahead, you'll have joined up with them by tomorrow night. Don't spare either yourself or the animals."

With the last words he leaped back into the saddle. He looked piercingly at the boy, as if to convince him of the seriousness of the situation by the force of his eyes alone. He could not have said how wretched he felt at having to leave those children behind like that.

"When your father wakes up, tell him he's got a good son," he called over his shoulder. He thundered off, while John stood looking after him, flabbergasted.

Deep in thought, John went and yoked the oxen. Poor brutes, they had a hard haul before them. And he would not be gentle with them—any more than he would be gentle with himself, or with any of the others.

It was an exhausted young driver who, after a journey of two nights and two days, approached the emigrants' camp near Soda Springs on Bear River as night was falling. Only a small corral stood there; John counted no more than twelve wagons. Evidently the caravan had disintegrated even more, and the others were still farther ahead.

He saw at once that it was a splendid camping place. The water of the river murmured enticingly, the several hundred head of cattle grazed greedily on the luxuriant green grass, and the hills round about were covered with the most beautiful fir and cedar trees. A spring spouted deliciously fresh water.

John's eyes, which, during the journey, he had hardly been able to keep from closing, suddenly opened wide to take in the wondrous sights before them. But it was not only the beauty around him which gave him such a queer feeling. It was—such a relief that they were among human beings again, that there was someone there who might be able to help Father and Mother and Indepentia, that, at last, he would be able to sleep.

On the edge of the camp he reined his oxen in,

and asked whether perhaps the doctor was with this troop, or, if not, whether there was a woman who knew anything about nursing sick people.

"Ha, John Sager!" someone cried, and Mr. Ford came running up. He started at the sight of the boy's utterly weary face.

"Is the doctor here?" John repeated his question impatiently.

"Yes—that's to say, if you mean the vet. . . ."

John nodded. He was too tired to say one word more than was necessary.

"Bring him here. Please! Father and Mother are very ill. For two days now, Mother's been too ill to feed the baby, and I can't get her to take anything else. We've tried to feed her on sugar and water and cow's milk."

Mr. Ford went trotting off to fetch the doctor.

John looked thankfully after him. He felt too exhausted to go a step further himself. He remained sitting on the driver's seat, his elbows on his knees, and his head in his hands.

His drowsy eyelids were beginning to droop again. All the sounds he heard seemed to come from a great distance. He felt Francis come and sit beside him. Louise was busy in the back of the wagon. She was trying to soothe Indepentia, who was crying pitifully. Yesterday she had screamed loudly all day, but evidently she no longer had strength left for that. "Quiet now, quiet now," he heard Louise saying, as if she was very far away from him.

The sound of men's voices startled him into wakefulness. There came Ford and several other men. Others were following. The doctor was walking in front. With his long legs, he jumped up beside John and into the wagon. John wanted to follow him, but the doctor sent him away.

He sent the children out of the wagon. In the twinkling of an eye they were sitting beside each other in a row on the grass. No one said a word; all waited in suspense.

It did not last long. The doctor came out. He did not look at John and the other children. And it was with difficulty that he spoke when he said to the waiting crowd, "They're dead—both of them, Henry Sager and his wife."

"It's not true, it's a lie!" John screamed.

He leaped at the doctor and repeated his words, screaming, shouting, crying. His throat felt as if a hand were round it, strangling him.

"It isn't true, it isn't true!"

The doctor seized his hands, but he tore loose

and tried to climb into the wagon. Two or three compassionate hands pulled him back. Then he threw himself on the ground, and buried his head in the cool, moist grass; he bit it, to prevent himself from bursting out crying again.

Father and Mother dead! Father, whom he could not do without, and Mother, dear Mother, with her gentle face and dark, deep eyes. Mother's shoulder with Indepentia's little head on it!

That child! What was to become of that tiny child? It was as though a mountain came rolling over John, a burden so heavy, so impossible to lift, that he felt as if he was suffocating.

A smothered sob was forced up from his throat. He tried to lie quite still, but his shoulders began to shake, his whole body trembled, something gave way in his throat, and the sobs came jerkily, shudderingly, one after the other.

"Father and Mother," he cried, "Father and Mother. . . ."

Suddenly he felt a hot little hand on the back of his neck. Without looking he knew it was Matilda. Little Matilda. Comforting, caressing—and she was only five years old! He was nearly fourteen!

He had to do the comforting. It was his duty to look after the others, to help them. He did not dare to look up yet. For a brief while longer he let that little hand do its soothing work. There was something singularly calming about it. Little Matilda . . . touched, he looked up at last. She looked at him, and her hand slid caressingly down the arm with which he was now leaning on the ground.

"John, please stop crying," she said.

John knew she was right. He had no right to cry. He was the eldest. He had to be a support for the others.

He sat up, and stretched out his hand. She laid her cheek in the hollow of it, and then she began to weep. Big quiet tears.

Cathie and Lizzy were both crying in long sobs. Cathie because she realized that Father and Mother really never would wake up any more, ever; and Lizzy because everyone else was crying, and everything was so strange. Two women took the little girls away with them.

Up till then, Louise and Francis had been sitting quietly weeping side by side. Francis had angrily shaken the pitying hand of Mrs. Ford from his shoulder. Now they got up, and both walked with dragging feet and tears running down their cheeks to John and Matilda. They sat down beside them.

No one ventured to disturb the children for the time being.

As quietly as possible two women and a man climbed into the wagon to prepare the dead couple for burial. After brief consultation, it had been decided to bury them that same evening. That would make it possible for the children to sleep in their own wagon for the night. Moreover, the caravan had to be on its way again early the following morning.

John looked somberly on when Mrs. Ford went off with Indepentia in her arms, wrapped in Mother's purple Sunday shawl—just as on that first day. The baby had stopped crying now; she must have fallen asleep.

John himself also fell asleep . . . at last. He lay in the grass, and Francis and Louise combined efforts and rolled him up in a blanket. He did not wake up.

The caravan traveled on.

By now, it was but a small column of ox wagons which made its way across the superb wild mountain country en route for Fort Hall, a British fur traders' post. Before them, two columns had already turned off to the southwest—California was more attractive to settlers than Oregon, where obstruction from the British was to be expected. But in both cases it was necessary to travel through difficult mountain country.

John sat on the driver's bench, Louise beside him. They were responsible now. They had not said one word about it, but they both felt it that way. Francis and the others accepted John's authority.

Francis rode on horseback behind the cattle.

"Tough little devil," said the other herdsmen, approvingly. They had respect for those Sager children.

On the evening of the second day—they were due to reach Fort Hall on the morrow—John was called before the small council of representatives which ruled all such wagon trains. In this council was vested the executive power to which everyone had to submit. Admittedly, anyone could speak and plead his cause before this assembly if necessary; but there was no appeal against the decisions it took. You had to accept them. That was an unwritten law.

Louise gave him a clean neckerchief, and before he left the wagon she solemnly handed him Father's hat. She considered that John had a right to wear that now. In silence he settled the big hat down on his ears. In silence he betook himself to the council, which was sitting in a semicircle in front of a big campfire. John felt that danger threatened him in some way, and he was resolved to stand firm.

The oldest of the men motioned to John to sit down on the ground along with them. Then he cleared his throat, taking longer to do it than was necessary, and began.

"We may as well go straight to the point, lad—it's no good beating about the bush. You children can't stay together. A household made up of kids, all by themselves in one wagon, runs too great risks. So we've divided you among three families. You and Lizzy are to go in with the O'Connells, Louise and Matilda along with the Mullers, Francis and Cathie are coming with me, Indepentia will stay with Mrs. Ford. That's the best way of arranging it. I hope you agree."

It was all John could do to let him finish. He realized that a lot depended now on his keeping calm. He had to be as much like Father as possible. They had to have confidence in him. His fingernails were pressed tightly into the palms of his hands. He knew that Father and Mother would think it terrible if they did not stay together, not to speak of what he thought about it himself—and the others. . . .

"Sir," said John—he didn't know how else to begin—"I realize that you think it's best that way. If I was you, I might think so myself. But if I did, it would be because I didn't know the children well enough. I mean, you don't really know us so terribly well. You don't know how good Louise is at washing and baking bread and—and all sorts of things; she's had to do them long enough already for Mother. And Francis and Cathie can look after our cattle very well. Cathie always has a stomach-ache if she's got to do something; but we're strict with her, and we can't complain. I can handle the oxen and horses, and I can shoot and hunt, too. Father always said, 'You shoot mighty well, John, for a boy of your age.' I'm not so young either. I shall be fourteen next month."

He stopped and glanced round the circle of men.

They sat looking kindly at him, but he could not see that clearly in the unsteady flickering of the flames. The lad was remarkably like his father, they thought—in the slow, judicious way in which he spoke, and also in his gestures, which had a certain power of conviction. John Sager inspired confidence. That again was exactly what his father had always done.

He wasn't stupid, either, for he cunningly added, "I think Lizzy and Cathie would be *very* troublesome if they were to go to other people . . . and we want Indepentia back," he ended resolutely, carrying the war into the enemy's camp, and thus employing the best tactics without knowing it.

The men looked at each other, pushed their hats to the back of their heads, sucked at their pipes— in short, they pondered deeply. Young John Sager was someone to be reckoned with.

"We'll let you try to stay together," was the decision. "We'll see how things go. But the baby stays with Mrs. Ford."

CHAPTER 5

The Children Alone

In southeast Idaho in an area of barren wilderness lay Fort Hall.

It was a small, roughly built stone fort, where a few men of the Hudson's Bay Company traded in furs with the Indians, completely cut off from the rest of the world. The Indians brought hides and beaver skins; in exchange, the white men gave them tobacco, powder, lead, rifles, mirrors, beads, and, later, whisky. Fortunes were amassed in fur trading—all the top hats in the Old and the New

World were made from the silky beaver skins.

About halfway through July, in the year 1844, the little caravan of American emigrants with which the Sager children were traveling arrived at that British outpost. They were hospitably received there; but when their future plans came up for discussion, the factor shook his head.

The men were sitting in the fort's inner courtyard. Two Indian women were serving them with strips of roast buffalo meat, tender steaks of horse-flesh, and Indian "honey balls," in which whole legs, wings, and heads of grasshoppers were to be found. Glasses were clinked and healths were drunk, but nevertheless the atmosphere was not cheerful. As good British subjects and loyal employees of the Hudson's Bay Company, the factor and his men were hard at work trying to dissuade the emigrants from trekking on to Oregon.

The emigrants, tired out and already thoroughly discouraged, did not know that these warnings were addressed to anyone and everyone who appeared there with a covered wagon and intended to go and settle in Oregon. For the men of the Hudson's Bay Company, Oregon had to remain a fur trapping area, and perhaps, in the future, become British territory. Hence, American settlers were unwelcome. Once a sufficient number of American citizens lived there, the American Government would no doubt take the necessary steps to annex the no man's land of Oregon.

"You're taking wagons over the mountains to the Columbia Valley?" asked the factor, as if he could not believe his ears. "What's got into you, men? Don't you people know *anything?* Haven't you any idea of the kind of wilderness you'll land up in there?"

"Maybe . . . but Dr. Whitman got through with a wagon train last year, didn't he?" the obstinate Irishman, O'Connell, retorted.

"Whitman? I take my hat off to him. I've never met a man to touch that one! But not everybody can do what he did! And what was the price he had to pay, in human lives, in cattle, horses, and equipment? You don't know *that!*"

"But at any rate there's a trail now which we'll be able to follow, more or less," O'Connell persisted.

"A trail? You show it to me! What there was in the way of a trail has been swallowed up by the wilderness again, by snowstorms, sandstorms, avalanches. Man, what *are* you thinking of?"

"I'm thinking of trying it!"

"If you go too far to the north, you'll get lost in
a region of deep chasms, towering mountain peaks,
impassable passes. You've got to cross rivers; you've
even got to cross the Snake twice, and no party's
ever succeeded in doing it once without losing
people and cattle, because the current's so tremendously strong. Before you even reach the Boise
River, you have to pass through an area where
three or four Indian tribes have banded together
to bar the way to white men. They're beginning to get anxious about their precious hunting
grounds. And then, winter will have fallen before
you've made the Cascade Mountains.

"On the other hand . . . if you go to California,
to the southwest, the route's considerably shorter.
And easier."

The factor fell silent. That was a long speech,
for him; but it was not a speech he was delivering
for the first time. And, just as on the previous occasions, his words would bear fruit.

That night, a serious conference took place
round the campfire just outside the fort. The meeting did not last long, for agreement was soon
reached. They would follow the advice of the
British factor. The caravan would turn off south
to California, as those which had passed through

there before had done, according to the factor.

John, who was now allowed to be present at the gatherings of the caravan council, even though he was not allowed to say anything, sat chafing with indignation. They had got more than halfway, at the cost of many sacrifices and great exertions; they had lost people, cattle, wagons, and goods; and were they going to give up *now?*

Out of his grief for the loss of his father and mother, a burning desire had grown in him. For as long as he could remember, it had been his father's dream to possess a big farm in the valley of the Columbia River. John wanted to carry out his father's wish. If the others wouldn't go with him, he would go alone! He and his sisters and brother. *They would get there. The Sagers would get to Oregon.*

While the voices of the men buzzed around him, he solemnly took that resolve, in silence. Staring into the campfire with unseeing eyes, he pondered plans.

Early next morning he discussed his scheme with Louise and Francis. Francis agreed immediately. Louise looked concerned, but said she was willing, all the same. "It will be very difficult though, John."

"Yes, it'll be very difficult, but we can do it," said John, and clamped his teeth round the stem of Father's pipe, in which he smoked kinni kinnick, the ground-up bark of the red willow.

The entire day was occupied in secret preparations. They wanted to leave that same night. They had no time to lose. It went without saying that they would have to go secretly, otherwise they would be stopped.

They would leave the wagon behind. John chose their strongest ox, and their most robust young cow, to carry stores, weapons, blankets, and tent. They did not dare take the two horses with them for fear of the Indians, who would steal horses as soon as look at them. Possession of a horse was everything to an Indian. And not every Indian had one.

Louise piled in a corner of the wagon everything which she thought might be of use on the way. Flour and the last of their sugar, salt, bacon, dried and minced buffalo meat, a kettle and a pan, blankets and canvas, towels, the Bible, and sewing materials. John laid the rifles on the pile, with everything that went with them, ramrods, powder, lead, percussion caps; and the waterskins. He hung Father's big tinderbox firmly on his belt, and

Father's hunting knife, too. His own he gave to
Francis.

They did everything in an atmosphere of great
tension; they hardly said a word, or looked at each
other. They felt they were about to undertake
something risky, whose outcome was not certain.
But they would not admit it to each other.

At last there remained only two, very important,
things to be done. They had to fetch Indepentia,
and John wanted to get hold of a dog.

"Louise," said John, "give me Father's last tobacco and Mother's silver locket. There are Indians at the fort, and one of them goes around with
a nice wolf dog."

"D'you mean to say you want to barter Mother's
locket for a dog?" asked Louise sharply. It was
the first time she had come near to losing her tem-
per, but she was disappointed in John for wanting
to get rid of Mother's old locket on the little silver
chain, which she had always worn round her
neck.

"How do you think *I* feel about it?" John retorted roughly. It was because he felt so bad about
it himself that he grew angry. Louise ought to
realize that he wasn't doing it for fun. It was for
the safety of all of them that he was having to do

it. He could not stand on guard every night. And the dog would be useful in hunting, too.

Louise said nothing. She still could not see the importance of having a dog.

"Do you want the Indians to take us by surprise, or one of the children to be eaten by wolves or by a grizzly bear?" John asked impatiently. "Come on, give it to me!"

Still without saying a word, Louise took the locket out of the little bag of needles and thread which she had laid ready to be taken with them. She picked its little cover open with her fingernail, and took the miniature portraits out of it: a black silhouette of Father as a young man, and a drawing of John as a tiny boy. Then she shut the locket again and gave it to him. She gulped, and said, "I understand—but it makes me feel so bad, that's all."

John stowed it in his pocket. Suddenly he had the greatest difficulty in keeping back his tears. Nevertheless, he was glad that Louise and he found the same things sad and difficult, and the same things good and pleasant. He would dearly have liked to throw his arms round her neck; but a man didn't do that sort of thing. It was a long time since he had given anyone a kiss. It seemed as if Mother had been dead for ages, and yet it had only happened last week.

He turned his back on Louise with a jerk. "I think I'll go and fetch Indepentia first. I can see about the dog presently," he said brusquely.

Indepentia, at any rate, was something a man could hold in his arms without losing his self-respect. Of a sudden he was seized with an almost unbearable longing to press his cheek against her warm, soft little head.

He began to run. The wagon in which the Fords were living was right opposite theirs in the corral.

"Mrs. Ford, may we have Indepentia for this evening?" he began. "We haven't had her with us for so long. And we'll look after her well."

Mrs. Ford looked at him doubtfully.

"Oh, *please*," John pleaded. "If you'll let us have her this evening, and perhaps for tonight too, we'll give you a bit of sugar. Please, Mrs. Ford—we can look after her very well—after all, she drinks cow's milk now. We'll let you have two cupfuls of sugar."

He felt a wretched fraud. But he salved his conscience by telling himself that Indepentia herself would certainly sooner be with them than with Mrs. Ford. And, when all was said and done—Indepentia *was* theirs.

Mrs. Ford was terribly tempted by that sugar. But Indepentia Sager had been entrusted to her care; and suppose anything should happen to her! But the Sagers were such good, dependable children.

"You'll be sure to take good care of her, won't you, John? And remember, lad, don't give her pure milk. Put a dash of warm water in it."

"Yes, Mrs. Ford."

How excited the boy sounded. And how eagerly he stretched out his arms for his baby sister. She was no more than a little bundle, in his mother's shawl. That lock of black hair only just stuck out of it.

John repressed his grin of delight until he was out of sight of Mrs. Ford. Then he ventured to bow his face for a moment, and put his cheek against Indepentia's warm baby head.

"Indepentia," he whispered, "you're going to Oregon. Along with us. And you'll grow up in a lovely valley among flowers and bean poles and wheat and maize."

"I've got her!" he said, when he reached their own wagon, and lifted her up and put her into the outstretched arms of Louise, who bent down to receive her from where she had been standing waiting. Inside, Indepentia was laid down in her old place.

"Now I'm going for the dog!" John cried exuberantly, and was off in a flash.

He returned with a prize—a real wolf dog, perhaps eighteen months old. On his way back from the fort he had picked up Francis, whom he had sent to spy out the land early that morning.

"At first the Indian wouldn't do it, of course. But I'd kept back half the tobacco, and when I put that along with the rest, it was all right. I didn't even show him the locket," he said, with a sidelong look at Louise.

He was holding the dog on a leash. The animal was not accustomed to that, and when John tried to stroke his head he growled and showed his teeth.

Francis said shrewdly, "I guess that Indian thinks the dog will find its way back to him of its own accord. And then he'll have both tobacco and dog."

John shook his head. "We'll tie him up good and tight. And tonight, when we go, he'll run on the leash."

"He'll bolt off anyway when we're two days' journey farther," Francis prophesied.

"I'll shoot a deer and give him good meat to eat," said John. All the same, he was beginning to get a little afraid that his younger brother might turn out to be right. The bargain had been very easily made. And Indians were crafty.

John had caught sight of Matilda walking toward them. He wanted her to help him. She became close chums with every animal she came across.

She was toiling along, hugging to her little round stomach a much too heavy pot of batter belonging to a neighbor. But no sooner did she see John, with the dog beside him, than she was there in a flash. The pot with batter was planked down in the grass, and had been lapped up in less than no time by another dog, which came shooting forward. Mrs. O'Connell threw up her arms and screamed, but by then it was already too late.

Matilda stood right in front of John's dog and looked at him in a friendly fashion. She gently laid her hand on his head; he permitted the liberty. Then she dropped down on her knees in front of him, and put an arm round his neck. The animal sat down. They remained sitting beside each other like that for quite a while.

John gave the leash to Matilda. "You take him to the wagon," he said.

"What's his name?" asked Matilda.

"The Indian called him Shongsasha," John replied. "I thought we might call him Oscar."

"Oscar," Matilda whispered softly in the dog's ear. "Oscar."

"Go on, take him to the wagon," John repeated.

She got up, put her little hand on the dog's head, and walked to the wagon. "Come on, Oscar," she said.

The dog went along with her, the leash dragging behind him in the grass.

That night, Matilda slept under the wagon with the dog beside her.

More than an hour before the first rays of the sun were due to appear above the hills, the great adventure began.

The previous evening, John had told the younger children all about it, and had impressed them with the necessity of not making a sound when they left. Francis had reconnoitered the route. First they would have to go some distance to the southeast; then they would go round behind a hill, to reach the right trail, in a northwesterly direction.

In the wagon they were abandoning, John left a note:

I am on my way back with my brother and sisters. If we hurry, we shall still be able to go along with Kit Carson from Green River Rendezvous.

John Sager.

He could not have thought of a better way of putting the others off the scent. The children's tracks would lead eastward, and the note said why. If anyone were to ride after them, they would not be found anyway.

John loaded the ox and cow with the packsaddles and leather saddlebags from the horses, behind a clump of tall shrubs a short distance away from the camp. He succeeded better than he had expected in getting everything roped securely round their awkwardly shaped bodies. It was fortunate that the beasts were so docile.

When all was ready, John climbed into the wagon for the last time. That was a difficult moment. It was dark inside, he could hardly see an inch; but desolation assailed him from every dark corner. There at the back, Father and Mother had lain ill, and there they had . . . he swallowed and swallowed, he could not get rid of that lump in his throat.

"Good-by, Mother," he whispered. "Good-by, Father. We're going to Oregon. All of us."

With a jerk, he turned his back on the wagon and all that was in it, and in one jump stood on the ground, on the outside of the corral. Then they started.

John carried Lizzy on his back and Indepentia, warmly wrapped up, in his arms. Francis carried one rifle over his shoulder, and another in his left hand; with his right he led the ox by the halter. Louise led the cow, holding Matilda by the hand, and Matilda, in her turn, held tightly on to Cathie. Oscar the dog walked close at Matilda's heels.

They did not say a word, and walked as quietly as possible through the night, which was growing lighter.

The older children were laboring under violent tension; it was as if everything in them vibrated. And every sound made them jump. A dog barked; farther away an ox lowed and another answered; from the camp came the noise of a clanking chain; another dog began to bark. With their hearts in their mouths they crept on. The moon was low in the sky, and the stars were beginning to pale. Soon the sun would rise.

The first pink, pale light of dawn glimmered above the mountains in the east.

CHAPTER 6

Fight with the Bears

The Snake River cuts its winding course through the Rocky Mountains from east to west, across what is now the state of Idaho. The landscape there is wild, majestic, massive. Gaping chasms, bottomless canyons, steep mountain slopes, gigantic peaks, and in the lower regions, treacherous morasses and quicksands. Below the timber line, a wild vegetation through which it is often impossible to force a path; above the timber line, a bare, fantastically

formed mass of rock where only mountain goats
dare risk their lives.

Through that country, the children wandered.

And they really did wander, for all John knew
about the route was that they would have to cover
three hundred miles in a westerly direction through
the valley of the Snake before they reached the
fur traders' post of Fort Boise.

As far as possible, he tried to get down close to
the river and follow it, because there was grass for
the cow and the ox. But where the river flowed
away green and foaming through a canyon, whose
walls of rock towered up sheer from the water,
they had to leave it and climb up, and find their
way across the mountains.

Sometimes they came upon something that resembled a path; they did not know whether it had
been made by wild animals or by Indians, and
often the going was so difficult that only with the
greatest effort and with extreme slowness could
they make any progress at all.

And then thirst came to torment them. In the
baking heat between those gray rocky cliffs, sweat
poured down their faces; they licked their salt lips,
and became even thirstier.

"John, I've got a tummy-ache, and my throat hurts too," Cathie complained.

Plucky little Matilda trudged on in silence. Tears sometimes trickled down her cheeks; she licked them away, but tears are salt. She grew ashen pale under her sunburn, and John noted with concern the black rings round her big, dark-blue eyes. She gets to look more and more like Mother, he thought.

Little Lizzy started every morning laughing and skipping. She slept like a top every night; she was a source of comfort and amusement to everyone; she did not see danger anywhere, and the first and the last drop of water were for her, though she was also allowed to share the cow's thin milk with Indepentia. Anna submitted faithfully to being milked, but did not yield enough to allow everyone a drink, not even half a mugful.

Later in the day, when weariness began to tell on her, Lizzy grew listless, started to cry, until John, tired and thirsty himself but with lips clamped tight together, took her on his back and carried her for a while.

Louise walked without saying anything the whole day long. She never complained, but she never laughed either.

She was quite different from Cathie, who could sometimes be terribly tiresome, but a moment later could laugh and play about as if they were still at home on the farm, just as in the old days. In the freshness of early morning, when a film of dew lay over shrubs and trees, she would lick all the leaves.

Francis was John's greatest support.

He had not the strong body and muscles of his elder brother, but he was tough and tenacious and very courageous. Francis's courage was of the kind that lies deep in the heart. He remained cheerful and lively; without him, the load of responsibility would have weighed very heavily on John.

When the going was rough and steep, John would take the little bundle that was Indepentia out of the leather bag dangling on Walter's right flank—on the other side hung a leather waterskin—for he was afraid that Indepentia might be hurt if the ox fell.

But Walter never fell; how he did it was a mystery, but he always managed to keep his unwieldy body steady on those four legs of his, which looked so fragile. Now and again he did raise his head and utter a pathetic bellow, as if invoking the help of the cloudless blue heaven.

The cow was rather more agile, and quicker.

"Come on, Anna, come on, Anna!" Matilda would sometimes stand and call; and then Anna would come jogging across the rocky ground, almost skipping, with her heavy body, under which the limp udder dangled. She tore leaves off bushes with her rough tongue, and sometimes chewed bark like a mountain goat.

Nevertheless, grass was of vital importance to them all. Without grass the animals could not have stuck it out; and without the animals, the children could not possibly have carried all the baggage. Without the cow, Indepentia would have been utterly lost.

When it was possible, John tried to go down to the river, which flowed through a tortuous narrow valley for a great part of its course.

There it was green, grass grew, sturdy cottonwood trees with heavy crowns even stood there; but the brush was so dense, that John could cut a road for his little caravan only with the greatest difficulty. However, often it was in that very underbrush that they found tracks which they could follow—paths which had been made to and from the river by animals. When they found such a path, Oscar would always run on ahead, sniffing, and Matilda had to call continuously, in her high, piping voice, to keep him from bolting off.

Sometimes John could even smell the rank scent of some animal or other. He was always speculating as to what animals came along those paths, and what his little party might encounter.

There were many kinds of small tracks there. They might have been made by rabbits, martens, and opossums; the larger ones were perhaps the footprints of a wildcat or a lynx. John saw many tracks of deer and antelopes. He hardly dared think about grizzly bears, but he knew they must be there.

Down in the green dusk of the dense undergrowth, the children did not have to contend with that baking heat which gave them so much trouble up above. But it was stuffier, closer, and there were mosquitoes. And then, that constant rustling—it was swarming with game there, but the animals darted off as soon as they heard the party approaching. Very occasionally they would see the head of a deer or antelope peering inquisitively through the leaves, and then there would be a sudden loud cracking of branches as the creatures sprang away with timid leaps.

The children were startled by all those sounds,

particularly at first; but they got used to them. However, John always held his rifle at the ready.

Toward the end of a day's march, they were dragging themselves along, but John would not allow them to rest and camp much before sunset. He was so obsessed by the idea that it was vital for them to hurry, to reach their goal before the snowstorms began, that he was almost cruel to his sisters —but also to himself. When, during the last hours of the day, he hoisted Lizzy on to his back again and again, and carried her as long as he could, he sometimes felt as if his spine would snap.

One day—they had lost count of the date by then—they found, quite early, a spot which absolutely clamored to be used as a camping ground.

It was a big round open space in the middle of high underbrush; the grass was thick and green. A mighty silver spruce tree stood there, towering far above the shrubs and bushes, and its lower branches offered blessed dead wood, to feed the finest of campfires. The river flowed near; a path made by animals ran down to a watering place.

The children looked imploringly at John.

They were nearly weeping with weariness, they wanted so terribly to stay there, but it was still early, that they knew—the sun was not yet low enough. Would it be possible to soften John for just this once? Their feet were swollen and raw from walking, their boots pinched, everything hurt, they were more tired than they had ever been in their lives. . . .

"Oh, John . . . please!" Louise pleaded.

Francis never took his eyes off his brother. He was ready to obey any order he was given, but he wanted desperately to be allowed to go and lie on his back, and take off those chafing, torturing boots. Louise had an ointment for the open blisters. Only John and she knew that it was just ordinary rifle grease.

John said not a word, but he nodded.

The animals were already grazing; he began to take their heavy loads off their backs. He patted Anna on her neck, just as he had patted his horse in former days. "Good girl, good girl!"

He had to do something, otherwise he would collapse from weariness himself. But there was enough to do.

First he broke armfuls of dry wood from the silver spruce for Louise; never before had they come by their firewood so easily. Francis stacked it up, while Louise was already slicing off thick rashers from the last remaining meat of the buck which John had shot two days before.

"It's time you shot something, John," she said worriedly.

"Don't bother your head about that," said John.

He was right; game sometimes crossed right in front of the barrel of his rifle, when he went on alone for a short distance. But he had no intention of shooting wild creatures unless they were needed for food. Today they had reached that point. That was one of the reasons why he had agreed to camp for the night earlier than usual.

Camping was a great deal simpler nowadays than when they had still been traveling with the wagon train. Now, in actual fact, it only amounted to choosing a good place and making a fire. For the rest, everyone rolled themselves up in their own blankets; the little girls lay together like a row of sausages on a buffalo's hide, and the flanks of the party were formed by John and Francis. They took turns keeping guard and prodded each other awake whenever they could no longer keep their eyes open. Sometimes both of them dropped off to sleep, relying on Oscar.

John most preferred a spot beside the river. He would tether the ox and cow close to the bank, and the children slept between the river and the little

rampart which John built up every evening out of
the packsaddles and baggage. That gave him a feeling of greater security. And he saw to it that all the
rifles were kept loaded at all times. They never
pitched the tent, they were always too tired for
that.

Now, when the flames of the fire were burning
up, he left the children behind in the care of Francis and Oscar.

Francis carried two pistols on holsters at his
belt. They were much too big and heavy for him,
but he could handle them quite well, all the same.
Three loaded rifles stood upright against each other
behind the parapet of baggage. They were old-
fashioned muzzle-loaders; the ramrods lay beside
them.

John took the fourth rifle, the best and newest
they possessed, a breechloader, and went out on
the trail, carrying the powder horn slung over his
shoulder. He would have loved to eat one of those
hissing slices of venison which Louise was holding
above the fire, but he wanted to shoot more meat
first. Then that would be settled.

He did not need to go far.

Close in front of him on the narrow path there
suddenly stood a splendid antelope, with round,

gleaming eyes and quivering nostrils. The animal
held its delicate head erect, and stood stock-still.
John always found it hard to shoot down such a
lovely creature, but he had no choice.

His father had taught him to shoot right between
the eyes. He leveled his rifle, aimed, and fired at
the very moment when the antelope lightly flexed
its hind legs to jump away. It fell dead at once,
long shudders rippled across its skin—a beautiful
smooth brown pelt with a thick black stripe along
the back. The animal lay with outstretched legs.
It was a young buck.

John walked back to the camp.

"Francis! Cathie!" he called. They would have
to help him lug the antelope home. Fortunately,
the distance was not great.

Together they seized its hind legs and dragged
it to the camp; its head trailed lifeless and limp
behind.

John took his hunting knife, and with one sweep
cut through the jugular vein. The blood spurted
out, and Cathie held a pan under it; Louise always
cooked black puddings for them from fresh game.
She still had a little bit of flour left.

Louise started down the animals' path to the
river, carrying the leather waterskins. A translu-

cent green twilight hung there, and it smelled strange, almost rancid.

She came to the river, which flowed on broad and darkly gleaming, falling steeply as it went, foaming round projecting points of rock and round small, overgrown islets. She looked at the steep, dark northern bank on the other side. She looked to the right, to the east whence they had come; but the bluffs and mountain peaks were hidden behind the tall willow trees nearby. She looked to the left, to the west, first up at the mountains, and then down. . . .

There, in an inlet on a little sandy beach, an enormous bear with three young lay basking in the sun!

Louise's heart stood still. Her only thought was to get away, noiselessly, without the bear noticing. But she stood there as though paralyzed, she could not move for sheer fright.

A branch snapped. Slowly the bear lifted its head, looked round. . . .

Louise dropped the waterskins and ran, as fast as her bare feet could carry her. Behind her, the bear came splashing across the river, through the shallow water.

John was still busy with the antelope, when he

heard a penetrating scream, followed by another, and yet another—close at hand now. They came from the direction of the river—it could only be Louise. There she was—screaming, as she came tearing along in the strange green twilight between the willow shrubs. Behind her came a sound of cracking and snapping. . . .

It was a bear, a huge, reddish-brown grizzly, whose ungainly body thrashed along at breakneck speed through the green tunnel of the path, which was much too narrow for it. The brute was no more than ten feet away from Louise. Savagely it launched itself forward; Louise had reached the open space.

"John," she cried, "help me!"

The boy already had his gun to his shoulder, but he did not dare to shoot yet.

The she-bear was momentarily dazed by the sharper light, perhaps also by the campfire, and confused by the many children she saw there. She stopped for a second, reared up on her hind legs, and mowed the air with her formidable paws with their great, sharp claws—a hairy monster ready for the attack.

And now two young bears appeared behind her. Growling, with white teeth bared in a snarl, they lurched along behind their mother. Just as the bear had been put out by the sight of the children, so was John taken aback by the danger of three bears.

He only had one shot in his gun. He *had* to save the children. But he was not alone.

He fired . . . and at the same moment Oscar, the wolf dog, shot forward and flew straight at the great bear's shaggy throat, bit tightly into it, and would not be shaken off.

The bear tottered. She had been hit; where, John did not know.

Francis fired his two pistols, one after the other. A bullet struck the bear's left ear; dark red blood started to drip down its terrifying head. The monster roared, tried to get rid of the dog; there was a storm of white fangs and slashing paws, lightning swings, blows, and growls. The dog yelped, but held on; the movements of the bear became more sluggish.

The animal reared up, Oscar hung onto her throat; blood trickled to the ground from an open gash on his back.

Francis thrust a fresh rifle into John's hands and he fired a second shot, right between the little flashing eyes. The bear growled, gurgled, and fell forward, right on top of Oscar, who, howling, tried to drag himself out from under the great beast.

"Francis," John yelled, "give me another gun!"

Francis was already there.

It was high time, for the young bears were growling as they came nearer. They lacked their mother's lust for battle, but they smelled blood and they were deadly dangerous.

The animals moved slowly, and were close by —an easy target for a cool-headed hunter, but not for a trembling boy. John lifted to his shoulder the rifle which Francis had pushed into his hands, aimed, and . . . the first of the two bears fell.

Suddenly Cathie began to scream, and Lizzy joined in. At last the unbearable tension had begun to take effect. But it was disastrous, for John's attention was distracted, and that of the remaining bear was attracted. Snarling, the young animal shot forward and made for the girls.

Before anyone knew what was happening, Francis had torn his red shirt off over his head, and thrown it to the animal. Instinctively, he had made just the right maneuver. The young bear threw itself on the shirt, set its white teeth in it and tore the thing to shreds, worrying it until its curiosity had been satisfied. Then it lifted its head again.

But meanwhile John had seized the third muzzle-loader, and aimed once more. He fired, and now the third animal tottered on its feet. It fell to the ground only a couple of yards from Matilda, who had remained sitting where she was, white as a sheet, and staring fixedly. Big tears slowly welled up in her eyes, as she looked at the bear lying in its death agony.

John had dropped his arms to his sides; he stood looking dazedly at the three dead animals. He was trembling all over. A trickle of blood dripped off his chin. Without thinking, he wiped it away with the back of his hand and looked at his hand in surprise. Then he felt that his tongue was hurting; in the terrible tension, he had bitten too hard on it. He closed his eyes for a second, to shut out the light; he wished he could have closed his ears as well. He longed desperately for silence, for rest.

Francis was the only one to run forward to help Oscar, who was still lying, softly whimpering, with his hind quarters pinned under the dead she-bear. He repeatedly lifted his head, but it fell again at once. Matilda followed Francis with her eyes. Suddenly she saw him jump backwards and run off, looking distractedly about him. He darted up to the dismembered antelope and seized one of the

legs. With that in his hand he ran back. Matilda
looked in the direction in which he was running,
and saw a third small bear strolling at a leisurely
pace down the green tunnel of the little path.
Sniffing first on one side, then on the other, he
rolled peaceably along on his stumpy legs.

Before the animal reached its dead mother,
Francis threw it the blood-stained joint of fresh
game. Growling, the little grizzly shot up to it,
worried it; then set its teeth purposefully in the
meat again, turned round, and jogged back down
the path. It disappeared from sight.

John, whose attention had been drawn by Francis's running to and fro, looked on in silence.

"That was just as well. Not one of the guns is
loaded now."

"I knew that," Francis said calmly.

"Oh," Louise suddenly remembered, "the waterskins!"

"Where are they?" asked John.

"Down by the river," she answered, shamefacedly.

Without a word, John set to and loaded all the
rifles again, the new breechloader last of all. Then
he took it and walked circumspectly down the

path. A few minutes later he came back with the precious waterskins.

That day, the children dragged themselves on until deep into the dusk. None of them wanted to camp in the place where the three dead bears lay. When they left, vultures were already circling above the spot, black against the pale blue sky of evening. John and Francis carried the badly injured dog between them, wrapped in a blanket. He was a heavy, limp burden, and slowly blood seeped through the blanket.

They went more than a mile farther on. They had wrapped their swollen, cut feet in strips of red flannel from Francis's torn shirt. They all carried their boots dangling round their necks.

The undergrowth grew less dense. When they finally decided to camp, a narrow open valley stretched before them. Little streams dashed and splashed down from the mountain walls, and they fell asleep at last with the sound of the water in their ears like a comforting lullaby.

CHAPTER 7

Quicksand

They lost all count of the days. They walked and walked and walked. The nights grew longer, darker, colder.

In secret, John prayed that they would be able to stay down beside the river. As long as they could do that, they had grass and water at any rate. Game became scarcer. The mountain walls on both sides of the Snake grew more menacing. John eyed those towering cliffs in dread that a moment should come when they would be able to get no farther.

They were not hungry; he was still always able to shoot something. In fact, they had not even touched their store of bacon and pemmican yet. They did sometimes suffer from thirst, when, although close to the river, they had to toil along its high bank, without being able to get down to the water. But then they would sometimes find a little stagnant water in hollows in the rocks. They bailed it out into their waterskins, Louise boiled it in the kettle, and they drank the lukewarm, insipid stuff.

Oscar had made a good recovery after his fight with the bear. They had rested for three days after that adventure, had slept a lot and eaten a lot. It had done them good, but they had been on the road again so long since then. So terribly long. . . .

Walter grew visibly weaker, but he still carried his load with patient good humor. Sometimes he would sink to his knees, but then he would scramble up again and struggle gamely on. Round his neck his skin hung in slack folds, and his shanks almost stuck through it, as sharp as arrows. On his knobbly backbone he had open wounds where the badly fitting packsaddles chafed him. Louise smeared the spots with rifle grease every night, and John slipped dry moss under the straps when loading up.

Anna, the cow, got leaner, but also more lithe and quicker, and she yielded milk regularly.

Indepentia grew on it, even though it did not make her fatter. Her little face and hands were red and swollen from gnat bites; she would beat the air desperately and clumsily with her short arms, but she could not keep the insects away. At times she wailed piteously; but sometimes she slept for hours on end, for the greater part of the day. Her back and legs were red and sore, in spite of the rifle grease Louise smeared on them.

"I'm so afraid it'll be gone soon," she said once.

"That's nothing to worry about," said John.

That day he shot two mountain goats, and picked out the fattest parts. Louise melted them down and the result was a thick, yellowish ointment which stank but answered the purpose admirably.

The children grew thinner.

Their hair straggled over their shoulders, their clothes hung in tatters; Louise no longer repaired anything. But she tried to sew moccasins, as she had seen Indian women do. She used deerskin for the purpose, and sewed with sinews which she had previously chewed soft and split. But she made hardly any progress, the first pair had yet to be finished.

The children were still walking in their old boots. John had cut the toes off all of them; the children's feet were too swollen and painful for them to wear them normally. In fact, the only way of getting the boots on in the morning was to make them sopping wet, so that the leather became supple and soft. In the course of the day it got dry and hard, and at night, when the boots were pulled off, they sometimes took with them the skins of blisters which had burst in walking, dried, and stuck to the leather. That gave rise to many crying fits, and Francis never used so many long, strange words as when he was pulling off his boots. John was silent, as always.

The harder things became, the more severe he grew toward the children. They became frightened of him, and he noticed it. It hurt him, but he did not change his attitude. He *had* to be strict, otherwise they would get snowed up there in the Snake Valley before the winter came.

Night frosts were already occurring; at night they all huddled close together, each in his or her separate blanket, with the canvas of the tent over the lot. In the west, the mountain ridges were already covered with snow; the number of the white peaks constantly increased.

They *had* to get on.

John lashed them forward with threats and rough words. And they obeyed, for without John they were lost. But they grew frightened, all the same, and shrank from him. Even Francis did not always understand him. They did not see that he always demanded much more from himself than from them.

Of all of them, he looked the worst. His bleached hair hung round a livid, gaunt face, with eyes sunk deep in sockets surrounded by dark rings: his body was nothing but bone, muscle, and skin. But the children only saw that he looked stern and hard. Nevertheless, Matilda still sometimes felt for his hand, and she could look up at him with eyes which said, "Come, John, be nice! Laugh—just once!"

But he could not laugh.

Often he took Indepentia in his arms for consolation. He would walk on in front of the others, hugging the baby to his chest, his eyes looking into hers. The round, trusting eyes of Indepentia called out the best in John. He bowed his head, and sometimes tears dripped down on Indepentia's little face. He felt so lonely, and the task he had taken on his shoulders was much too heavy. Perhaps more than any of the others he felt a deep homesickness, a craving for the support and love of his father and mother.

The narrow, shut-in valley became marshier; it began to look like a swamp. For the feet of the Sager children, it was a blessed relief. Their shoes remained pliable and soft all day, and their feet cool. But the heavy pack animals found the going difficult.

One day, the valley began to broaden out. The sound of running water grew louder. It looked as if the mountains were moving apart.

At the end of a long day's march, the children stood before a narrow tributary which flowed into the Snake at a sharp angle. The strips of bank beside the river were broad and green; the water, which was shallow everywhere at the end of that dry summer, flowed swiftly into the wilder water of the Snake. There were forests of whispering yellow rushes, with dark-yellow feathery plumes, which glinted and became lighter in color when the wind ruffled them. It was much less forbidding and threatening than in the dark, narrow valley of the Snake.

"The ground's too damp for camping here," said John. "We'll go a little way back from the river, as far as those cedar trees under the mountain slope. Tomorrow we'll have to cross this. We've got to keep following the Snake."

They woke up feeling fresh and cheerful the following morning. John had been out very early and shot three rabbits; Louise roasted them, and sprinkled a tiny pinch of gunpowder on them—a wretched substitute for pepper and salt. But it was a delicious breakfast, all the same.

John went into the river first, in order to find the best place at which to ford it. In all probability, the water would not come higher than his knees, but he tied a rope round his waist and gave the end of it to Francis to hold. "You never know."

He walked across the boggy bank to the river, and cleared a path for himself through the dense reeds—carefully, for the edges of the leaves were as sharp as knives.

The bed of the river consisted of firm, grayish sand, which was hard and tacky. But no sooner did he stand still than it closed like a vise round his toes and heels. Quickly, he pulled his feet out, and shouted behind him, "Quicksand!"

He went on moving his feet up and down, and in that way made some slow progress. By now he was up to his knees in the water; it came no higher. "It's just about the same depth everywhere," he called back over his shoulder, "but the bed's probably all quicksand."

The children sat and watched him.

Constantly moving, never standing still for a moment, he reached the other side and tied the rope securely to a bush of red willow. Then he came back, and tied the loose end of the rope round a cottonwood tree on their side of the river. After doing that, he took his hunting knife and cut a wider path, with sweeping strokes, through the reeds which bordered the bank in a dense fringe. When he was finished his arms were bleeding from many fine, shallow cuts. He walked back a few steps and splashed the ice-cold water over them until they ceased to bleed.

He joined the others again. Louise looked at his arms. "Too sharp for the little ones," was all he said.

"Francis and I will carry the baggage across,"

he added shortly. "It'll be difficult enough to get the animals over unloaded."

Francis made the crossing through the icy water three times and John six times, heavily laden and never standing still for a second.

"Now, for the animals."

John made a soft clucking noise with his tongue, in order to coax them up to him. They came, full of trust. He patted their necks, stroked their noses.

Then he said to Francis, "Cut off a couple of stout sticks, will you?"

He continued to pat and stroke the cow and the ox. It was as if he wanted to ask their forgiveness in advance for what he would have to do to them.

When Francis came back with the sticks, his face set hard and tense again. "They mustn't stop for one moment," he said. "We've got to chase 'em along as fast as they can go."

"Let Matilda go to the other side first and call them," Louise suggested.

That was a good idea. John took Indepentia in his arms, Francis took the hands of Matilda and Lizzy.

"No," said John vehemently. "I'll carry Lizzy later. She'll have to wait, that's all. Don't forget,

Matilda, you must never stand still. Just go on moving your feet up and down, up and down; don't stop, not even for a second. And you've got to walk along beside that rope. If you feel the ground sucking you down, grab the rope. D'you understand?"

The child nodded. John was never really frightened on her account; she always obeyed him to the letter. She also knew, almost instinctively, what was dangerous and what not. Now she walked, kicking out with her feet through the cold water, which came almost up to her middle. She did not utter a murmur. They reached the other side in safety.

John and Francis splashed back behind each other along the rope. The sun was already high in the sky; hours had passed. John was tired.

Once on the bank, he gave his orders. "Louise and Francis, you two must take Anna and Walter by the halters; I'll follow behind with the sticks. Cathie and Lizzy, stay here till I come and fetch you."

The animals began to hesitate as soon as they reached the reeds, but a smart whack against the backs of their legs worked wonders. Once in the water they did not flinch; only when they noticed how their hoofs caught fast in the heavy, gripping sand did they become uncertain again. John never stopped hitting their legs, with both sticks, left and right. Francis and Louise pulled on the halters as hard as they could, ceaselessly trampling in the water.

From the other side, Matilda called in her high, childish voice: "Anna! Walter! *Come* on, now! Anna! Walter!"

The cow mooed anxiously, but things went well. And they continued to go well. Once they had passed the halfway point, John hardly needed to strike them any more. The flanks of the animals heaved with exertion, and with blind terror of a danger they did not understand. Of their own volition they did their utmost to reach the other bank as soon as possible. All five were immeasurably relieved when they climbed up it.

John would have liked to fling himself down on the ground, as he had done after he had almost got drowned with Charley in crossing the North Platte. But that was impossible now—he had more responsibilities than he had had then. At once he set out on the return journey. His feet, which at first had hurt from the cold, had now become numbed blocks of ice. And he was so weary that it was as much as he could do to constantly lift them up and set them down. But he got there.

He took Lizzy on his back, and motioned to Cathie to walk behind him. This time he did not repeat his warning that she was under no circumstances to stand still for a moment. To him it had become so obvious that he did not think of impressing it again on Cathie.

They stepped into the water. Lizzy was heavy. John labored on, without looking round. Suddenly he heard a voice calling him from behind, "John! John! Shall I catch you a lovely silver fish?"

He looked round. There stood Cathie, bending down over the water with hands outstretched, laughing.

Keeping his feet constantly moving, he stayed where he was, and shouted angrily, "Cathie, come here at once!"

She tried to come, but she couldn't. Great fear could suddenly be read on her astonished face. She pulled and pulled. She could not get free. Her feet were fast, as if in iron traps. The sand had already closed round her ankles.

"John!" came in a small, pitiful wail from her lips. "John, I'm caught!"

The boy, who had been red with anger, went as

white as chalk. "Francis!" he called hoarsely. "Take Lizzy over for me!"

Francis let himself down from the bank and ran into the water. The two boys rushed to meet each other. John set Lizzy down in the river and Francis seized her hand; they ran. At the water's edge, Louise was standing ready with something red that was supposed to be a shirt; at any rate it was dry.

In the meantime, John had reached Cathie. He threw his arms round her waist and pulled, tugged, pulled—as hard as he could. But he could not bring much force to bear because he had to keep his own feet constantly in motion. The sweat of fear stood out on his forehead.

"Ow, John, you're squashing me flat," Cathie panted.

"Be quiet!" John snarled. His brain was working feverishly. It was obvious that this was not helping at all. His strength was not enough. With lightning movements he began to haul in the slack rope. He fished the end out of the water, tied it three times round Cathie's thin little body, and made an enormous knot in it. Then he left his little sister alone. Without looking round he splashed off.

Immediately Cathie began to squirm and twist

in all directions. It was such a horrible feeling, round her feet, and it was so tight. The calves of her legs hurt as if someone was pinching them very hard. She twisted forward, to left, to right, back, tugging at her legs. Suddenly she lost her balance and fell over backwards in the water. John heard the splash, turned round with a furious face, and came back and helped her up again.

"Confound you, child, stand still, d'you hear?"

He trampled off once more, as fast as he could. He felt exhausted. It was as if hundreds of needles were pricking the muscles of his thighs. Finally, he climbed up that bank again.

The others stood waiting anxiously; no one said a word. Everyone looked on in suspense at everything John was doing, so accustomed were they to the fact that John always came to the rescue, always knew how to meet every situation.

He picked up the rope, told Francis to untie it from the willow shrub round which it had been fastened, and walked with it to the only sizable tree which was not too far away, on the highest part of the bank. He climbed up into it with the rope, selected the most suitable place where two main branches forked, cast the rope over the fork, and then climbed down again.

He called Walter. The ox looked at him, but did not come.

Matilda and Francis both walked up to him, and Francis seized the halter. Matilda tapped his dirty hind legs, softly. The animal swished his tail, but began to run. John did not even go to meet him, he was so tired. . . .

"Louise, the girth from the packsaddle!" was all he said. Even his voice no longer had any strength. He tied the broad strap round the ox's body, but left some play. The free end of the rope was tied to the strap. And then, "Pull!" John commanded.

He gave the ox a gentle slap on his angular shanks. Francis took the halter again. He led the animal away from the river. The rope began to tighten over the fork of the tree, with Cathie at the other end. The ox pulled, the rope was taut; the ox pulled even more, urged on by everyone.

Cathie screamed.

Nobody paid any attention. Of course Cathie screamed. As the rope tightened round her body, it felt as if she was being cut through the middle. But her feet were beginning to come free, albeit with tormenting slowness. In spite of the pain, Cathie suddenly became brave, and screamed as little as possible.

The ox went on pulling. He did not slacken off for a second, but the children on the bank could not see that it helped and Cathie could not tell them. She felt as if she was being torn in two. She no longer stood, she half lay in the water; she did not feel how cold it was, her hands were clenched convulsively round the taut rope.

The children on the bank looked on in desperation. It did not help at all, they thought. No matter how hard Walter pulled.

"Cathie!" Louise shouted from the edge of the water. "Try harder, or you'll die!"

"I'm not *going* to die!" Cathie screamed back in smothered tones.

They were so used to contradicting each other that Louise almost shouted, "Oh yes, you are!" But she checked herself just in time.

Cathie was now lying on one knee in the water, with her other leg stretched out behind her. She could feel that the foot of her outstretched leg was almost free. And the other was very nearly as loose, though now the sand had also got a hold round her knee. She was still pulling as hard as she possibly could on the rope; when she did that, the loops round her body did not hurt so much. Louise stood wringing her hands at the river's brink.

The ox pulled steadily on.

Suddenly he plunged forward. The rope was no longer taut and vibrating. Cathie was being dragged through the shallow water. "Whoa!" shouted John, and Francis pulled the animal back by his halter. Walter stood still.

Half-choked, Cathie scrambled to her feet, dripping wet. Sobbing, she splashed toward land, where hands were stretched out to pull her up. Oscar ran to and fro along the bank, barking loudly and wagging his tail.

"It was awful—it was *so* awful!" Cathie got out, in a trembling voice, between sobs.

There was a dry towel handy, there was sun, and there were warm hands full of bunches of dry grass. But that was not enough. "Make a fire!" John commanded.

Everyone went to look for wood except Louise, who remained with Cathie. Even little Lizzy was picking up twigs. In a very short time there was a big heap, and the fire was blazing up high. Cathie basked in the warmth; the color came back to her face. She laughed, those comical dimples reappeared in her cheeks, and she shook her long curls like a wet poodle.

"So you see, I *didn't* die!" she suddenly said to

Louise. It sounded almost spiteful, but they all laughed. That was Cathie all over: spiteful and cheerful, bubbling with high spirits, touchy, full of rebellion, full of unexpected co-operativeness. That was Cathie, and that was how they liked her. They had never realized it so clearly as now.

Everyone looked gratefully and gladly at John when he said, "We're not going any farther today. We'll stay where we are."

But no game came within range of his gun, and they had to break into their stores for the first time. John did not like that at all, for he feared that the day would come when they might need it more than they needed it now. But when he saw the happy faces gathered round the bacon spluttering in the pan, he smiled wearily. It didn't matter—the important thing was, they had got Cathie back again.

CHAPTER 8

Pursued by Fire

Endless days of journeying. Walking, walking, walking.

Would there never be an end to it? Would they never get anywhere? It all seemed so hopeless.

John hardly dared to look at the line of wretched, thin children's faces straggling behind him. No jokes were ever made now, no shout of laughter ever went up; even Cathie and Francis were silent.

They walked and they walked. On feet in which

knives seemed to be sticking. On swollen legs. With hollow cheeks and necks like sticks above clothes which had been torn to flinders.

One of the worst things about the grueling march was that Indepentia became filthy. They could no longer keep her properly clean. Her little face and hands were swollen and red from insect bites, her eyes had become slits. Nowadays she cried for hours at a stretch, but they did not even hear her, they were so used to it.

At night, when John looked, in the light of the campfire, at his brother and his little sisters sitting there exhausted, hungry, often thirsty—then he felt almost distracted. He had done all this to them. So now he had to take them on, to the bitter end. He had to—he had to. . . .

They were still following the Snake, but the valley was growing more and more difficult to traverse. The banks of the river were high, rocky, steep; for more than a week now, it had been impossible for them to get down to the water, although they constantly heard it rushing by.

The few places where water had collected in the hollows of rocks were the children's only salvation. Usually it was Oscar who found them. With his nose to the ground, he followed the tracks of the animals who went there to drink. Whenever he found water, he would bark. And John and Francis could not run up quickly enough with the waterskins.

The little troop dragged itself on. They always had rags wrapped round their feet now; they tore into strips their last reserve in the way of clothes, in order to do that. Round those strips, they wound strips of fur from the animals John shot. But he did not shoot much these days. Even the wild creatures avoided that inhospitable region.

John had ordered Louise to go extremely carefully with the stock of food. But she had not been careful enough for his liking, although the children often went to sleep hungry. Then he had taken the matter of rationing into his own hands. And since then they had found him even sterner and crueler than before.

He had received the first and only pair of moccasins which Louise made. He had them because, as a rule, he walked three or four times the distance which the others covered, either reconnoitering or hunting for food. But the moccasins were also worn quite through already; he had wound strips of buffalo hide round them.

John felt the dumb rebellion of the older children growing. The little ones accepted the life they were leading, no matter how terribly they cried sometimes. They knew no better, they remembered practically nothing of other days; even Matilda had forgotten everything, she had become a real child of the wilderness. Exhaustion, hunger, and thirst had erased all earlier impressions from their minds.

But it was different with the older ones. They were capable of feeling a poignant homesickness for former times, for life with Father and Mother, for life at home on the farm and later in the cosy security of the ox wagon. They remembered only the good things, and not those things which had made life difficult at times even then. As far as Fort Hall, it had been easy all the way, they thought; but after that. . . .

They did not reproach John at all. John longed for them to do so. Oh, if only they would reproach him with all the things with which he reproached himself: his stubbornness, his stupidity, his short-sightedness in embarking on this plan. Then he would have been able to defend himself—then he would have told them about Father's burning desire that his children should grow up in those blessed valleys on the other side of the Rocky

Mountains. And about Indepentia, who had to be christened by Dr. Whitman.

So they went trudging on. In silence.

With fear in his heart, John saw that the valley seemed to be coming to an end—that high mountains seemed to bar the way to further progress. It was possible that the river entered a canyon there, through which there would be no road that they could take. And what then? Go back? But that too was quite impossible. Did the others share his fear? He did not know. They said nothing.

There came a day when it looked as if they would have to leave the river. Broad clefts cut through the high bank. Ferns and bushes grew there. They had to make a detour. John told the others to wait, and went on ahead.

The nature of the ground forced him toward the southwest. The murmur of the waters of the Snake sounded softer and softer. He was getting steadily farther away from the river which they had to follow at all costs. But he had no choice.

Then he heard a new sound of running water, coming from the other side. Suddenly, as he turned the corner of a cliff, he saw a white, foaming cataract a hundred yards in front of him. It was a narrow stream, gushing down in a bed much broader than itself, between two mountains. Beside the stream, through the long grass, ran a distinct and fairly wide trail.

It was not impossible that wagons had come through there, long ago. But it was as clear as daylight that it was a trail made by animals, Indians, and trappers!

His heart leaped up with gladness. These were signs of human life, of new prospects. The stream flowed to the Snake River. The trail continued to follow it. To the left and right, mountain slopes rose.

John ran along the track as fast as he could. Soon he no longer heard the waterfall, but instead, the water of the Snake. The trail ran straight toward the river. There was a wide open space which had probably often served as a camping ground. Traces of old fires were still to be seen—patches burnt bare, from which sun, wind, rain, and snow had still not yet been able to disperse the old gray ash completely.

It was obvious that here, above the mouth of the stream, there was a ford, and that the trail continued on the other side. And it was hardly possible for it to lead anywhere except to Fort Boise. There could not now be so very many days' journey left.

John walked back. When he reached the place where he had discovered the waterfall, he sprang quickly up the slopes. Over and over again, he stopped and whistled. And once he fired his pistol straight into the air, out of sheer joy.

A doe jumped, startled, out of the undergrowth. He whipped the pistol back into the holster and aimed his rifle. . . . The animal halted and looked round; John saw a small dappled fawn lolloping unsteadily along behind her, its nose cocked up at an angle. He had not the heart to shoot. He lowered the barrel of his rifle. There were sure to be more wild animals around there.

When he got back to the others, they hardly recognized him. He looked happier than they had seen him look for weeks.

"I've found a trail," he said simply, "and there's game here, too. And we're going to cross the river."

The latter prospect was not so very pleasing to the others, but John's cheerfulness gave them some courage, all the same.

That night they ate rabbit and venison—as much of it as they wanted. There was plenty of clean, fresh water, a glorious campfire was burning, they were not cold, and they all went to sleep with full stomachs.

Next morning Indepentia was given a thorough clean-up. She screamed heart-rendingly as Louise softened the crusts of dirt with hot water, and bathed her face with cold water. John, who otherwise never wasted a minute, stood looking on like a perturbed young father. Good Heavens, how filthy that child was! And how thin she had got since the last time he had looked at her properly! Her red-scrubbed skin clung to her little ribs like a film, but her stomach was round and swollen, in contrast to her sticklike legs. She had sore patches on her body which could not be got clean.

After breakfasting on venison, they crossed the river without any trouble. The water of the Snake ran swiftly, and there were projecting spikes of rock round which it boiled and eddied wildly. But it was shallow, it was easy to wade through at that point, and much less treacherous than the apparently harmless quicksand stream of which they had such dreadful memories.

It was a wild, overgrown path which they followed after that, but it was very definitely a path. The way had been chosen well through that ever-

changing country; they climbed steeply, the trail
wound about continually.

One difficulty about which no one said anything, but which began to worry them more and
more, was that they went farther and farther away
from the river. And nowhere did they find any
standing pools. Their stock of water was small.

The animals suffered most. The dog, the ox, and
the cow all walked along with their tongues hanging out of their jaws like strips of dry leather.
Walter, the ox, was the worst off of the three. He
had already fallen twice in clambering up the
rocks. The cow tore like a creature possessed at
anything green she saw. She still continued to yield
milk—enough for Indepentia and Lizzy.

But after her bath Indepentia had fallen ill. She
vomited up everything she was given; it was terrible to see that wretched little heap of misery. She
cried weakly but constantly, and sometimes, when
she slept, John was seized with dread that she
might be dead.

Things went on like that for three days. By that
time, the last waterskin was only half full. Louise
doled out the water in a spoon, under John's super-
vision. He was more severe than ever. They all
had swollen and cracked lips, over which they

constantly ran their tongues; it only made matters worse. Their tongues also became swollen and painful, and their throats were parched.

"If we haven't found any water by tomorrow night, we'll go back to the river next day," said John tonelessly.

The others had wanted to do that before, but John had refused to listen. How would they ever get any farther, if they did that? They would not be able to take up any more water from the river than they had done to begin with. But now he too was forced to consider going back, even though he knew that if they did their case would be as good as hopeless.

That night John prayed for water. He prayed with a bursting heart, more passionately, more urgently than he had ever prayed before in his life.

Formerly he had prayed because his father and mother had taught him to. He ate and he drank and he slept and he prayed—he prayed because it was the thing to do, it went with all the other things. After Father and Mother died, he had forgotten all about it. He had seen Louise do it once or twice, but that had not lasted long either. They had become so engrossed in other matters.

But now—suddenly he had thought about it, he

did not know how it had risen in him so suddenly, like a ray of hope in the terrible darkness. Now he got down on his knees, some distance away from the others and with his back to them, and prayed.

"Great God, give us water. Give us water! We're so thirsty. Good God, please!"

Still kneeling, he collapsed forward, his hands on his knees and his head on the hard ground. All he had strength for was to go on whispering: "Water, please! Water. . . ."

They slept that night, all the same, they were so worn out. When they awoke they felt as if their tongues were sticking to the roofs of their mouths. They swallowed and swallowed, their throats seemed about to crack.

The sunrise was a vivid scarlet, and there were strange wisps of cloud in the sky. The landscape through which they were now passing was more open than it had been. They had climbed high. To the east and north the dry Snake Plateau rolled away, in peaks and valleys; to the west the chains of mountains were higher, and here and there white with snow. John measured with his eyes the distance to the nearest snow-capped peak, but he knew he had not the strength to get there. Snow

. . . melted snow was water. His tongue scoured over his cracked lips once more.

Around them the vegetation was parched and dry—some short, almost brownish-yellow grass, some thistles, and farther away a complete tangle of thick-leaved cactus plants.

The cow walked round them. Now and again she pricked her nose on the spines.

That gave John an idea. He walked up to the cactuses, cut the spines from the fat, fleshy leaves with his knife, and took a leaf back with him for each of the children.

"Here's a sweet to suck for everyone," he said huskily, in a clumsy attempt at a joke.

But it was not so silly as it sounded.

They all began to chew the leaves. They chewed hard and long, and they got some juice in their mouths, besides a stringy, rather bitter-tasting mass of pulp. It really did help!

John went back to the cactuses, and cut off as many of the spines as he could, to enable Anna to eat some of the leaves. He tried to get Walter there, but the ox lay gasping for breath, on his knees, and would not get up. So John cut some leaves off for him too, and took them to him; but Walter did not touch them, only looked at John with wretched eyes. Walter was nothing but skin and bone. Poor creature. . . . Oscar did not feel like a meal of cactus, either. The children chewed and chewed. John looked at the sky. Those wisps of cloud were peculiar. They were getting bigger and bigger. And there in the east, where he looked out over a barren chain of black mountain peaks, the heavens remained red. Strange . . . the sun was already too high in the sky for that.

Last night it had begun to blow, and as John stood facing the southeast against the wind, he felt that it was blowing harder, even harder. And then, perhaps, would there be rain? Were they going to have a storm? Was that the significance of the wisps of cloud?

Gradually they were growing more like clouds of smoke—thick, feathery monsters, which came nearer and nearer but still clung to the horizon.

He noticed that the animals were beginning to get restive. Even the listless Walter raised his head into the wind, and sniffed the air with dilated nostrils. Over and over again.

John glanced at the children. But for them nothing existed in the world apart from their thirst and their rebellion against the day's march ahead of them. John could not stop looking to the east; he did not understand what that could be.

Meanwhile, he began to break camp and pack. Francis helped him a little. But Francis had not much strength. Poor Walter had to be beaten to make him stand up. John would sooner have beaten himself.

It was as if a mist was rising with the ever more strongly blowing wind. But that was no ordinary mist. The children began to cough. They thought it came from thirst. But John knew it did not. He began to believe that he knew what was going on yonder.

A tremendous forest fire was spreading across the mountains, across the valleys, from mountain peak to mountain peak, blazing across the Snake Plateau.

The wind was blowing towards *them.*

The mist, which was really the precursor of dense smoke, became more and more stifling. At last the children noticed that it was smoke; their eyes began to smart. Nevertheless, they could still see nothing in the way of flames.

The fire was still too far away. But John knew what was bound to come. Now they would not be able to go back to the river, even if they wanted to. He whipped his little caravan forward. He could hardly get them to move. He swore as only the coarsest men among the emigrants had done. He dealt out blows right and left, shoving Matilda and Cathie on with a hard hand. This time he had given Anna a heavier load to carry than Walter, even though she was their milk provider. Walter could hardly keep his own bony body upright on his four weak legs. John took Lizzy on his back. And they went on. They walked and walked.

They walked with dragging feet, without complaining. They did not even have the spirit left to complain. John often looked behind him. The children coughed more and more often. The stinging and smarting of their eyes also grew worse. The cloud of smoke became more dense.

"It smells like real smoke," said Matilda, whose senses were the most sensitive of them all.

John nodded.

"But where's the fire, then?"

John made no answer. He thought, You'll be frightened soon enough when you see it.

Very fine flakes of ash, and even extremely small sparks, were beginning to blow over their heads. But there was still no fire to be seen. It was burning behind the horizon, but it must have been a fire along a tremendously broad front. If the wind did not drop, or if no rain should suddenly come . . . what then?

"John—look!" squeaked Lizzy's husky little voice, from up on his back. Rabbits were running past them, fleeing in the direction in which they were walking. There'll be more animals coming soon, thought John.

It was not long before they felt the ground behind them shaking. They could not see far through the smoke; suddenly three huge animals loomed up, tall and broad, galloping along, with enormous antlered heads. The male, with the largest antlers, led the way. Then came the female, and finally a young one, not much smaller than the female. Elk! They tore past, making for the west.

More animals were passing—they could hear that from the ground; but they saw next to nothing any more.

The rain of sparks became heavier. Behind the smoke, the ruddy glow became brighter. If they could have seen farther, they would have been able to make out the flames now.

What are we to do, John thought desperately, what in Heaven's name are we to do? All the animals are running, but we can't go so fast. If we were only above the tree line, where there's no longer grass covering the naked rocks, the flames wouldn't be able to reach us. But to get there we have to go higher, and the path doesn't rise.

They were still following the trail, which could be easily seen, even now.

"We're leaving the trail," said John. "We've got to go straight up the slope."

No one objected. What would have been the use, anyway?

They climbed and climbed.

John no longer walked in front. He had told Francis to go straight upward, no matter what came in the way. He himself walked behind, to chase and chivvy his little troop on. Forward— forward! He did not care now whether anyone moaned or wailed.

No, that was not true . . . he cared terribly. But he cared even more about something else. They had to escape from the fire.

He told them what was at stake. Then perhaps they would walk better, he thought. He put it bluntly and roughly. "If anyone wants to get burned, they can sit down and stay here."

They climbed.

They had seen no more trees for a long time past; there were still bushes, but they were so stunted as to be almost dwarf bushes. The fire was coming nearer. The smoke was growing stifling. It was like a red curtain. Behind it, the flames roared. The burning dwarf fir trees flared. Shrubs, dry grass— everything was consumed by the red flames. Farther on everything became black ash. John estimated the distance they had still to traverse as a mile. How much time had they still? An hour? Two? It all depended on the strength of the wind. In the last hour it had not increased. It seemed rather to have slackened a bit. God grant. . . .

They climbed, panting, coughing, sneezing.

Oscar ran round and round all of them, with his tongue hanging out of his mouth; Anna, who was carrying Indepentia, scrambled gamely along. John was so grateful to her that he felt a warm surge of love for her, almost as if she were a human being. Now and again, he patted and stroked her shanks. Walter, alas, had to be driven forward with the stick—mercilessly. It was the only way of saving him. But it was heart-rending to hear him gasping. His breast wheezed, sometimes he bellowed as if he was in his death agony.

On, on.

Lizzy became an unbearably heavy burden.

On, on.

Bare, rocky patches began to appear on the ground, but they were no more than small islands amidst low vegetation. Still, it *was* a beginning.

Higher, higher.

Now they could not see more than a few yards in front of them. The tears streamed from their smarting, red-rimmed eyes. The red glow behind the curtain of smoke was terrifying. For some time past they had heard a strange rumbling; now that it was closer, they could hear that it was the roaring of the flames.

"I thought we were dried up," Francis coughed, panting. "But I'm sweating like a sponge!"

Bare, rocky ground, with a few tufts of grass in the cracks—they could not see whether this place of refuge was really big enough. Just a bit farther, John urged them. Come *on*, now—please! Just a little bit! The ground remained bare and rocky. If we don't suffocate in the smoke, we'll get away with our lives here, thought John. Are we all here?

"You can all lie down now," he shouted.

Everyone was there.

No, Walter wasn't there.

John called, Francis called, Matilda called. No Walter.

"I can't go and fetch him," said John. "I can't see a finger in front of my face."

It was no longer possible for them to get away from the smoke. They all lay flat on their stomachs, with their hands over their eyes, ceaselessly coughing, raucously and hoarsely.

Then a gentle rustling note suddenly sounded above the roar of the flames. Drops of water fell! Raindrops! Big raindrops! And it did not stop at a few. A downpour came that was as if the heavens had opened.

Is this the answer to the prayer I said yesterday? John thought.

It poured, it fell in torrents, they were soaked through.

The smoke cleared. Farther down, a cloud of fumes hung about; but the rain soon put an end to that as well.

It would be impossible to imagine a sight more desolate than that which then met their eyes. To the south and east everything was black, black, black, as far as they could see. Many square miles must have been burned out. Here and there the short stump of a dwarf tree still stood.

The children lay on their backs, their tongues stuck out to catch the drops of rain.

John went across to Anna.

He unbuckled the baggage, and ran with Independentia's traveling bag to a sheltered place under a big overhanging boulder. Then he opened wide the two waterskins, the kettle, the pan. He took off his shirt and spread it out on the rocky ground; everything in the nature of a piece of cloth he spread out, and he called to the others to do the same. Francis, who at once understood why, did it immediately. Presently, when the rain stopped, they would again be without water, and what would happen then? If they could wring out their clothes, at any rate they could have something, even if it was only an inch or so at the bottom of the waterskins. But perhaps there were also hollows in the rocks in which puddles would remain.

Now they had to look for Walter. Walter also had waterskins on his back.

They espied him lying among some bushes, a big, formless heap, not more than fifty yards below them. John leapt down.

"Walter, Walter!" he shouted.

The animal did not even lift his head. God be thanked, the fire had not reached him either. It had stopped a couple of hundred yards away.

John came to him. He looked at him. He patted him, stroked him, walked round him and saw his eyes.

The ox was dead.

Slowly, John walked back to the others, carrying the waterskins. "Walter's dead," he said.

Nobody answered. The children went on drinking, catching the rain in their mouths, in their open hands; they sucked their wet shirts dry.

A feeling of dull misery came over John.

"Walter's dead!" he shouted.

That startled them. They stared. They stared down the slope at that pathetic heap of bones and skin which had done them such invaluable service on their way. Cathie was the first to begin to cry.

Matilda said, "Walter didn't get burned?"

"No," said John. "He fell, and then his heart stopped."

"Yes, Walter's heart stopped," said Matilda.

With John, she was the only one who was not crying. For even Francis was rubbing his eyes.

Of a sudden, Cathie began to laugh. "Do you see how black we are?" she exclaimed. "And Francis is getting stripes all over his face!"

Then they all had to laugh, whether they wanted

to or not. They looked so strange, with black faces and red, bloodshot eyes; and where the tears trickled down, they left faint, wavy streaks.

"John," Louise asked timidly, "John, don't you think we might risk cutting off a few slices of bacon?"

"Bacon?" said John.

All the same, it was no wonder Louise thought about eating. They were hungry! Now that their thirst had been quenched a little, they noticed it for the first time.

"Bacon? Walter's there too, isn't he? But no— I'd sooner. . . . If you'll just be patient, I'll go and shoot something. So many animals have been hunted out of cover by the fire."

He set to and dragged all the baggage out of the rain, which was still falling in buckets, into the shelter of the overhanging rock.

"Hey, give me a hand, all of you!"

Thank heaven, the powder had kept dry in its box. He charged the breech-loader.

"You make a fire there. There's enough dry wood down below."

He pointed to a broad, deep fissure, running at an angle into the side of the mountain and shielded by a massive boulder. They had a magnificent cave there. It couldn't have been better.

Having given his orders, he set out.

"Come on, Oscar!"

He climbed higher, for he not only wanted to shoot fresh meat, he also wanted to spy out the land. The edge of the rock terrace they were on blocked out part of the view. They had to find that trail again.

The dog began to bark, violently, almost anxiously.

From its bed on the ground, a catlike animal suddenly sprang up with a lightning leap, glistening wet. A lynx!

John shot it.

It was a female. Then the male must be somewhere about, too, he thought, for lynxes are always in couples. He reloaded his rifle as quickly as he could, and looked keenly about him. He heard a rustling of wet twigs and leaves. Prowling along like a big cat, the male went up to the dead female—sniffing, with green, flashing eyes.

John fired for the second time.

The animal fell on its side; it was not quite dead. A moment later John fired again, between the eyes this time. Wicked claws, those animals had. Its flesh would be tough.

John climbed a little higher, to where a point of rock stuck out. He gazed to the west over the mountain landscape, in the gray rainy light. His eyes remained fixed on one point, traveled farther, but returned to the same point. Always back to that one point, while his mouth slowly opened.

That . . . there . . . yonder, far below . . . that plume of smoke . . . and that—that square gray block beneath it . . . yes, it *was* a square, even though it was hardly visible against its surroundings in the rain-filled air.

That . . . that must be Fort Boise.

Fort Boise lay in the fork of the Snake and Boise Rivers. He could not see the rivers. But that meant nothing. They might be hidden in folds in the ground. That square, with that plume of smoke, *must* be Fort Boise.

In a flash, he turned and ran down the slope, past the game he had shot. He waved his arms; his long, disheveled, wet hair flapped behind his head.

"We're close to Fort Boise," he exulted hoarsely. "Two or three days off! Louise, Francis, *say* something, for Heaven's sake! We're close to Fort Boise. They'll help us there. There . . . why don't you *say* something?"

He stood in front of them, dripping wet, with his naked torso gleaming and his ragged leather trousers sticking to his legs, and his arms outspread. They were sitting huddled beside each other in the shallow rocky cave, behind a small fire that smoked rather than burned. They were hungry. They were not allowed to eat any bacon. They had lost the power to be glad.

Louise smiled at last through a mist of tears. "That's splendid, John. But we're so tired. And when we get to Fort Boise, we've still got to go on, haven't we?"

In spite of himself, John understood: they were too exhausted to rejoice about anything. However, a couple of hours later the atmosphere was better.

"Lynx is the nicest meat I've ever eaten," said Cathie, pulling at the tough roasted meat with her white teeth, for all she was worth. "The very nicest!"

Night fell. And they went to sleep. John kept the low fire going; he had got used to waking up constantly, throwing wood on such a fire, and dropping off again at once. Some distance away, wolves howled. Oscar lay half-waking, half-sleeping.

Next morning they went on their way.

Walter remained behind alone.

CHAPTER 9
Fort Boise

One afternoon in September, 1844, a boy stag-
gered in through the gate of Fort Boise. In his arms
lay a child.

The boy was dressed in nothing but a pair of
buckskin trousers, which hung round him in tatters, and two bundles of rags, which had once been
moccasins, on his feet. His hair, bleached almost
white, hung in tangled skeins over his bare shoulders.

The factor of that one-man post on the Snake

River was used to all the hard aspects of life in the wilderness. He had endured privations himself, and he had seen others endure them. But when he saw John Sager, words failed him: he could do nothing but stare in horror and amazement.

John's first question was whether there was a white woman in the fort. And that almost made the factor laugh. A white woman! The idea! No, there wasn't. Why?

John jerked his chin toward the little heap of rags in his outstretched arms. "She won't drink anything any more. She brings it all up."

The man examined the bundle more closely. With a feeling of repulsion, he waved away the flies which swarmed down on it. Was that red, swollen, wretched little object a child's face? Its tiny neck looked like a stick; and when he saw its grimy, skinny little carcass, with the abnormally bulging round belly, he could not utter a word.

"Perhaps there's a woman who'd be willing to suckle the child in the Shoshone Indians' camp," he suggested.

But privately he thought that no Indian woman would consider taking in such a terribly neglected child. He looked at the haggard boy, and the lad's eyes gazed straight and firmly at him.

"No, not an Indian woman, I can't rely on them," said John, who was hardly able to stand on his feet. "And besides, we've got to go on."

"On?"

Yes, of course they had to go on, they couldn't stay there; the factor was the first to agree with him on that.

John turned, and looked up in silence at the ridge of the hill down which he had just climbed. The factor's eyes followed his. And one shock was succeeded by another. There came the rear guard! Sakes alive! How was it possible!

A dark boy, about eleven years old, lean as a skeleton, led the little caravan, which seemed to consist of a horde of little girls in such a state of filth and neglect as the factor had never yet seen even amongst the poorest Indians. Round their dirty, skinny bodies hung colorless shreds of material which might once have been red; wherever he looked, he saw big eyes in emaciated faces with swollen, cracked lips.

No wonder, thought the factor. Those children must have suffered horrible thirst. They came from the bone-dry lava waste of the Snake Plateau.

He bawled something incomprehensible back

over his shoulder, across the inner courtyard of the fort.

An Indian came up, and the factor pointed to the little procession of children, which was approaching the gate with dragging feet.

"See they get something to eat and drink," he said brusquely.

The Indian stood rooted to the spot, looking with open mouth. White children on foot through that desert! He shook his head incomprehendingly.

John turned to Francis, who was now hobbling in. "There's no white woman here."

With difficulty Francis answered, "Then we'll have to do it ourselves, with Anna."

The factor heard a dog barking. Shortly afterwards the head of a cow appeared above the brow of the hill, and then the whole cow came into sight; she was loaded and hung about with baggage like a mule. The dog ran round and round the cow, for she made no progress. Over and over again she discovered fresh grass. In their burning impatience to reach the fort the children had not waited for her, but Oscar, whose herder's instinct had developed on the journey, had remained behind with her.

"What else have you people got, besides a dog and a cow?" the dumbfounded factor inquired.

"Have you got a father?" There was no mother, that was obvious.

John shook his head.

"Where do you come from, and how?"

"From Fort Hall, on foot."

Yes, where on earth else could they have come from? But it was impossible! The factor scrutinized from head to foot that brown, bony boy with the child in his arms. A lump came into his throat, and tears into his eyes. The boy filled him with deep respect; his body might be wasted and exhausted— but that firm chin, that resolute mouth!

"Sir," John asked politely, "may we stay here for the night?"

Stay for the night? Sakes alive, suppose they *shouldn't* be allowed to stay there for the night! The factor nodded his head vigorously.

"Boy, you can stay here as long as you like, and rest and eat and sleep. Heavens above, how's it possible! Come on, children, wash and fill your bellies, and sleep for three days!"

He pushed them in front of him, one by one, into a spacious, dark room, where a trestle table stood in front of an open roughly cemented hearth. A couple of crude chairs stood there, and the rest of the furniture consisted of packing cases and whisky barrels, which, when necessary, could serve as seats. In one of the corners lay a pile of skins. Rifles hung on the wall.

Oscar came running in wagging his tail, and Anna very nearly crossed the threshold.

"I take my hat off to that cow. Has she toddled along with you the whole three hundred miles?" asked the factor. He felt he had to say something, but he didn't know what; those children put him out, with their great, serious eyes and famine-ridden faces. He wanted to have everything done for them, but he didn't know where to start.

"Where may we put our baggage, sir?" asked John.

"Chuck it down anywhere, chuck it all down here!" cried the factor, walking quickly to and fro. "And you children go and sit down, too, for goodness' sake. Don't stand on those shaking legs! Heavens above, what am I to do with you? What would you like? What would you like first, lad?"

"Water, sir."

The factor went outside and shouted something. The Indian who had been the first to appear, and who proved to be the fort's cook, came up carrying two heavy earthenware pitchers. The water in them was cool.

The clear water dripped into the mugs through a little spout. The children fell on it. More—more, still more! Outstretched hands!

"Out of the question!" said the factor. He shook his bearded head. "You've arrived safe and sound, we're not going to make you ill here! Steady on, steady on!"

He looked at John, who was standing to one side. "Hey, lad, shall I hold that baby for you for a minute? Then you'll be able to drink too!"

"Will you be *very* careful with her, sir?" John asked earnestly.

The factor took the roll of rags. What a stench! He turned his head away. John saw it, and went red with shame. He gulped down a cupful of water, and took the child back from the factor.

"She's very ill, sir. She fell ill after we'd given her a really good wash, for once. For some time before that, we hadn't had enough water to do it. My eldest sister would like to clean her up properly now if, perhaps, we could have a tub of warm water." He checked himself, swallowed, and said with difficulty, "And then . . . then we'll just have to try her with cow's milk again."

"Do you think weak, lukewarm beef tea would be any good?" asked the factor, smitten by a brain wave. He felt unutterably ridiculous in the role of nursemaid. He coughed and scratched behind his ear, in his thick, black thatch. "And as for that tub —I'll see you get it!"

There was a separate washroom. An enormous barrel full of water stood in the middle. And a dozen big wooden tubs stood leaning against the rough log wall.

"When I get an invasion of trappers, they haven't the patience to wait for each other. They all want to wash at the same time," said the factor, who did not let the children out of his sight for a moment, as if he feared they might walk out through the gate again in that state.

"Splash around to your heart's content, here are scrubbing brushes and soap—it's not good, we made it ourselves out of bear's grease, but I don't suppose you're choosy. Throw your rags down in a heap; we'll burn the lot. I'll dress you up in new things; the girls must just not be too particular, that's all. The Company'll probably not take it amiss of me if I squander a few less pairs of trousers and blankets on the Indians in exchange for skins. And if they do take it amiss, I don't care.

"Lordy, Lordy, what a sight those feet of yours are! Hey!" he shouted through the open door of the washing room, into the sunny courtyard, where an inquisitive Indian was sitting on the ground before the threshold. "Hey, you—" and there followed a flood of vehement, incomprehensible words.

The Indian got lazily to his feet and slouched off to the other side of the courtyard, where he disappeared in the dark storeroom. He came back with an armful of moccasins. Only men's sizes.

"Better than nothing," said the factor, "and quite a number of these children's feet will have to be treated with ointment and wrapped in bandages, anyway. We'll freshen you all up. You've got a nerve, you kids, to cross those mountains! I wish I could spare a mounted messenger to send to the English factor at Fort Hall, to tell him you've arrived.

"Come on, there, scrub your arms! Hey, you, rub that other one's back! Little pups! You can't even wash yourselves properly, and you stroll around the Rocky Mountains!"

The children let the storm of words pass over them unheeded. It was nice to see a grownup again, and hear him, even if he did make as much uproar as a child.

Lizzy was taken in hand by Louise. She

screamed at being washed, and lashed out with
arms and legs. Of all the children, she looked in
the best condition. She had suffered least.

Indepentia was wrapped in cloths drenched in
oil. When the crusts of dirt had been softened, she
was bathed in lukewarm water. It was a long business, but the result was a great deal better than
what they had achieved on the bank of the Snake.
John, who stood by waiting, in an old blue soldier's
uniform with the trouser legs and sleeves turned
up, got her back clean in his arms. He looked as
proud as a father who sees his own child for the
first time. Solemnly he stepped across the courtyard with her. He felt reborn; the blood pulsed
strongly through his veins again, and he was as
hungry as a wolf. Now they would get food.

The Indian cook brought in big dishes of meat.
The children fell on them like little animals; they
did not even take the trouble to sit down. Lizzy
crawled up onto the table; but Louise found that a
bit too much. Holding some meat in her right
hand, she lifted Lizzy off with her left. Lizzy,
screaming indignantly, landed on the floor, where
she remained, gnawing away at a chunk of meat
like a puppy dog.

John stood a little to one side, and looked on;

with one hand he held a big lump of meat, and with the other he held Indepentia.

The cook brought beef tea in a bottle. With infinite patience, John fed it to the baby in drops. Half of it she brought up again. He was busy with her for over an hour. Then she fell asleep.

John looked at the factor. "We must get on again as quickly as possible," he said.

"Leave the baby and your two youngest sisters behind in the fort for the time being," the factor suggested.

But the boy shook his head. One thing was certain—they had to reach Dr. Marcus Whitman's missionary post as soon as possible.

"You're crazy," said the factor. "That child may die at any minute."

John went red with sudden anger, and said something he should not have said. But in a flash he clapped his hands over his eyes, and began to sob bitterly. The factor turned on his heel and walked away. The lad's tears were more than he could face.

The Indian who had brought the moccasins came in with some wood and lit a fire. Outside, the sky above the courtyard was flushed red; the sun was setting.

When the children had eaten their fill, they crept onto the pile of buffalo hides in the corner, furs were spread over them, and in less than five minutes they were all sleeping as if they would not wake again for years.

John and the factor sat in chairs in front of the fire. An Indian woman had come in and sat down against the wall. She was sewing moccasins.

"I've told her to make moccasins for all the little sore feet of those sisters of yours," said the factor casually. "She's my wife."

"We really shan't be able to stay that long, sir," said John. And he thought to himself: a white man with an Indian squaw. . . .

The factor must have read his thoughts, for he said, "All the trappers have Indian wives. They're at least as good as white women."

John thought of his mother's white shoulder, with Indepentia's little dark head against it in the dim light in the wagon. Strange—that it should be just that picture which would always remain in his memory. He said nothing.

"What do *you* know about Indian women?" said the factor, interpreting his silence incorrectly. "Shall I tell you a thing or two about 'em?"

But John had fallen asleep. The boy had slipped half out of his chair.

The man took him up and carried him to where the rest of the family lay, under the furs in the corner. He carried him as he might have carried a small child, muttering one rough expletive after the other below his breath. He tucked him up like a mother, pushed the stiff, unyielding hide under his back, murmuring, "Tough little devil! God grant that you and the rest of that small fry have a better future in store for you. Amen."

The children stayed at Fort Boise for five days. Five days and nights of eating, drinking, and sleeping.

It was remarkable how quickly they recovered. Their feet healed up; hard scars and calloused patches remained, but that was all to the good. Indepentia could keep milk down again; her cuts and wounds had closed, a new, purple-red, tender skin had grown over them.

Anna had been scrubbed and currycombed, and once more resembled an ordinary, robust cow.

John now saw the future in rosy colors. Too rosy —they still had to cross the hazardous Blue Mountains and at an unfavorable season of the year: it had grown too late. But the factor had promised to let him have an escort of three friendly Shoshone Indians, and horses.

And he had given John a map.

On the inside of a smooth, supple lynx's skin, the factor had charted the country: the course of the river, the mountain gorges and passes. He had roughly marked out the route with a piece of charcoal. "Here, and there, and then again, here—and *here* you've got to look out. Seek shelter in time when snowstorms break. Camp early and carefully every night, and move as quickly as possible by day."

John nodded. After all, with horses and an escort it would almost be a pleasure trip.

The factor read the overconfidence in his eyes, and said, "Never forget that bigger chaps than you, hard-bitten mountain hunters with good equipment, have gone into the Blue Mountains and never come out again."

John mentally classified this among the other tall stories told by the factor. He did not know what difficulties still lay ahead.

That night, the factor of Fort Boise told him his yarns for the last time.

"Did you see Jim Bridger, when you stopped at Fort Bridger?" he asked.

John shook his head. "He wasn't there. He was out beaver trapping."

"I can well believe that. An old hand like him can't lay off it. He's often been here. He's explored this country as no other man has, he loves the wilderness of prairie and mountain with all his heart and soul. I'll tell you a tall story about Bridger. In the winter of 1830 it snowed and snowed without stopping for months on end. For seventy days, Jim said. All the buffalo which had no shelter perished in the snow, but their bodies were preserved by the cold. When spring came, hunting was unnecessary. All Bridger had to do was pickle the frozen animals in the Great Salt Lake, and there was enough salt buffalo meat for himself and all the Indians in Utah for years. . . ."

The sun rose in a golden autumn mist above the Blue Mountains next morning, when the little caravan left Fort Boise. John went in front with one of the three Indians whom the factor had sent along with them. The boy was clad in buckskin from head to foot, and looked like a small, but nevertheless genuine, trapper. The other Indians held the reins of two packhorses, both fully laden. Louise and Catherine walked, but Lizzy and Matilda sat together on top of one of the packsaddles, tied like Indian children. Francis brought up the rear with Anna. Oscar ran to and fro, or trotted along beside Matilda's horse.

The factor had done everything he could to give them the best chance possible. All the same, he trembled for them.

He accompanied them on horseback a short part of the way. When the sun stood some distance above the mountains, John shook his hand in farewell. He would have liked to express his gratitude for a thousand things, but all he could say was, "Thank you very much!"

"God bless you, boy. Remember me to Marcus Whitman," said the factor.

That night he wrote a letter to his old mother at St. Louis. As a rule he only wrote twice a year —when the trappers called in at the fort on their way to the East after the summer and winter trapping campaigns. But he felt an urgent need to unbosom himself in his own language, to someone other than his Indian wife.

He wrote: "I've told you many remarkable things in my letters, but I've never had such a hard nut to crack as in these last days. A terrible story it is, but something unforgettably impressive. That boy —that John! . . . He was anything but an easy leader for them, he excused nothing. When his nine-year-old sister refused to hold the baby, he put the little girl across his knee, and gave her such a thrashing that she begged and implored him to *let* her hold the child. He had to be severe, his task demanded it. . . . After they'd had a rest of some days, I sent him further on his way under the protection of a few reliable Indians and with fresh horses." *

The children waded across the Snake River. The water was icy cold. Soaking wet, they went on. A chill wind blew from the northwest. Their route lay to the north.

It was not long before John's overconfidence sank into his boots. He saw how much effort it cost Cathie and Louise to keep up with the party. But it was impossible to make their Indian guides and escort stop. They strode on ahead, singing monotonous chants with long-drawn-out, droning notes.

* This letter is still in existence.

"Make them understand they've got to go slower, John," Francis urged.

"I've tried to make them understand that many times already," John snapped.

"Try again then!"

"Oh, John, *please*," Louise implored. Her legs were like lead.

Cathie was holding Anna by the tail, letting herself be half pulled along. "If you don't stop doing that. . . !" John threatened her. "It's difficult enough for Anna anyway, and without her Indepentia's done for."

Cathie reluctantly let go of the cow's tail. She walked with lagging steps.

"Come on, we mustn't fall behind," John cried.

He shouted to the Indians. They did not hear. He tried to catch up with them. He fired his rifle. That helped. With irritated faces they paused until, panting, he reached them.

With despairing gestures, he tried to make it clear to them that the children could not possibly move so fast. He threw out his hands and held them palms upward, to signify powerlessness. He pointed and gesticulated toward the ground: sit down, take a rest, I'll fetch them while you're waiting. He pulled at his feet, and made a painful face;

he panted and gasped and pointed to the stragglers: can't you *understand* how tired they are,
how heavy their legs feel, and how their hearts
thump in their chests?

The Indians did not understand at all, or pre-
tended not to understand. They wanted to get on,
that was obvious. This journey with a pack of neglected, orphan white children was an affront to
their self-esteem. The Father of the Fort had ordered them to take the children over the passes of
the Blue Mountains, and then return. Very well
. . . they would do that, after their own fashion,
and they would return as quickly as possible. Even
so, the business would take weeks, and, if they
didn't hurry up they would be overtaken in the
mountains by snowstorms. No . . . they didn't care
for this trip at all. And they didn't care for those
white children, either. They looked at John in silence, shrugged their shoulders, and walked on
again in silence.

John seized the pack horse, which one of them
was leading, by the halter. That suited them perfectly. Let the boy lead the horse if he liked.

The animal was heavily laden, and in front,
across the saddlebow, the three muzzle-loaders
were tied. John was carrying the breechloader;

the three Indians were unarmed. Francis was
walking behind, leading the second horse, on
which Lizzy and Matilda were perched on top of
the baggage, with Indepentia dangling at its flank
in her traveling bag.

The caravan went on. Jauntily singing, and with
swift feet, the Indians raced far ahead. The children dragged themselves along, but John no
longer harried them forward as he had been doing.

The trail was broad and easy to see. It led
through wild, high hill country. The afternoon was
waning; the sky in the west was already beginning
to turn red. One of the Indians looked round. The
children were not in sight.

They stopped. They were satisfied with the
progress made that day. They would wait for the
young whites and pitch camp. They sat down in
the tall, stiff grass.

Suddenly, the sound of trampling hoofs was
heard. John came trotting up on one of the pack
horses, from which the baggage had been unloaded. He was holding the reins in his left hand,
and a pistol in his right.

With the barrel of the pistol leveled at the Indians, he motioned to them to stand up. Stupefied,
they complied. He pointed to the south, and inti-

mated that they were to get going. He turned his horse until he was riding behind them. In that way he drove them back to the spot where he had left the children.

The Indians did not sing now. They walked with sour faces, and very slowly. John did not goad them on; he did not want to make them more ill-humored than was necessary. If the journey had to take place in this way, it would become difficult enough as it was.

They camped.

That evening, and throughout the whole night, John and Francis took it in turn to keep guard; they had their weapons with them in their sleeping bags.

Next morning the journey continued, with John on horseback and armed, behind the Indians. If he had not needed them as guides—and that *was* necessary, for the trail had already forked twice— he would have preferred to go on without them. The escort system had turned out differently from what the factor intended.

The other horse was now more heavily laden, and Anna had also been given part of the burden originally on John's horse.

There was no lack of food and water. The Indians set snares for animals, and foaming brooks and splashing streams dashed down from the steep hills.

The slopes were densely, darkly forested; here and there tall cedars and silver spruce trees stood out in bright contrast to the other evergreen trees. The weather was damp and dull. At night the little party crept shivering into their sleeping bags. John found the night watch more difficult each time. His vigilance relaxed as the days went on. The Indians were strangely impassive and detached.

The trail crossed the Snake for the second time, after another track had branched off to the southwest, toward the Humboldt River, in the direction of California. If possible, the water was even icier than it had been on the last occasion. They had cramps in their feet. This time they lit a fire after making the crossing. The Indians had respect for John, not only on account of the arms he carried, but of his whole personality, which compelled respect, young as he was.

For three whole days they followed the eastern bank of the river again, but at a comparatively great distance away from it; their course lay somewhat more to the north. John knew that they could not be far away now from the vast marshes and the valley of the Grande Ronde.

On the evening of the third day, they saw seven blue-gray plumes of smoke rising behind a distant chain of hills in the northeast.

Francis saw them first.

"An Indian village," said John.

"Or a trappers' camp?"

"Not at this time of the year. And they wouldn't light seven fires, either."

Their three guides had also noticed the smoke. They did not seem surprised, but pointed to it with vehement gesticulations. One of them began to tear up tufts of dry grass. He put them on a stick and, at a suitable moment, ran to the highest nearby hilltop, and lit his torch there. The grass torch did not burn long, but it was evidently long enough.

It might have been twenty minutes later when a loud yelling was heard, and three Indians on ponies appeared on that same hilltop. The Indian guides down below gestured to them. They signaled without words. The riders above galloped three times round their hilltop in steadily widening circles, and then vanished.

That night John did not feel easy as he sat beside the campfire. He was not frightened, for it was obvious that the horsemen they had seen, and consequently also the inhabitants of the Indian village, were friends or relations of the three guides, and, although the latter were cool toward the children and not very friendly, the atmosphere had become better rather than worse, owing to the respect they now had for John. He cherished no illusions; he knew that even though he constantly mounted guard over all the firearms, those three Indians, with the help of their fellows, could easily slaughter the entire little troop of Sager children.

But he trusted that the influence of the Father of the Fort would continue to be effective—after all, the Indians would have to be able to look him in the face again; and, moreover, he knew that children's scalps were not valued by Indians. For these reasons, he felt fairly safe. He did not believe that any downright evil plans had been made.

In that belief he finally fell asleep, tired out. He had seen that the Indians were asleep, and he had the rifles with him in his sleeping bag.

He was awakened by someone violently shaking his shoulder. He heard Francis's voice. "Wake up, John. They've gone off with the horses."

"Who?"

"The Indians. With the pack horses. We've nothing left!"

John was awake in a flash. He could not say a word.

Francis was now lying with his ear to the ground. "You can still hear their hoofs," he said. "What on earth are we to do now?"

"Throw some wood on the fire and make some coffee," said John, getting to his feet. "I'll go and look in the snares to see whether there's anything for breakfast. The girls will have to sleep on for a bit."

"There isn't any coffee. And there's no kettle either. There's nothing. Everything's gone."

John looked around. It was a fact—those scoundrels had taken the horses with everything that was on them. The children had nothing left but their rolls of blankets, their weapons, and their drinking mugs, which lay, together with Independentia's feeding bottle, in the trodden-down grass beside the smoldering fire.

John clamped his jaws together. But what on earth *was* he to do? He walked round the fire, kicked viciously in the ashes.

"Those moccasins have got to last a bit longer yet," Francis observed.

John could not help laughing. Little Francis sat there so pertly erect and resolute. And suddenly John felt grateful to him. He walked up to Francis, pulled him to his feet, put his hands on the slightly built lad's narrow shoulders, and said, "I don't know what I'd do without your help, you wretched little brat!"

Francis colored with pride and pleasure.

The future did not look so terribly black to the boys. "We've only got the Grande Ronde Valley and the Blue Mountains ahead of us, that's all," said John.

The society of their Indian escort had irked them more than they had cared to admit to each other. Now, at any rate, that load had been lifted from their shoulders. Admittedly, the fact that they also had to do without the horses, the store of food, and all sorts of other things was bad, but they had been much worse off than this. They were not hungry, they were not thirsty, they were wearing good clothes, they had weapons, and they were healthy.

"Where's Oscar?" John asked abruptly.

Francis went pale. They called and whistled. They walked aimlessly around. Oscar was not to be seen.

"They've taken him with them, of course!" John exclaimed. "The whole lot's gone to that wretched Indian village where we saw the fires smoking yesterday."

The girls had been awakened by their calls to the dog. Cathie was the first to perceive that their camp seemed less populated than usual. She looked sharply about her, and then asked hopefully, "Are they gone, those nasty men?"

"With the horses," said John.

Louise opened her eyes in alarm. "*What's* that you're saying?"

"The Indians went off last night with the horses and with almost all the baggage. They've stolen everything. And Oscar's gone too."

Louise realized the consequences of this and tears came to her eyes, but she said nothing.

Matilda and Lizzy, who slept together in one sleeping bag, sat bold upright side by side, with eyes like saucers.

"Has Oscar really gone?" Matilda asked.

"Now what d'you think? That I'm joking?" John snapped back. He minded terribly that the dog was gone, but, as always, he wanted to show it as little as possible.

At that moment a loud rustling sounded, which

came quickly nearer through the underbrush on the slope where they had camped. Before they realized what was happening, Oscar came bounding into the midst of them.

He shot straight toward Matilda and buried his nose in her lap. His tail beat the air like a pendulum gone mad.

Matilda bent her little body over the big dog, threw her arm round his neck, and said, "Oh, Oscar! You came back!"

John surveyed his little troop. He could not help laughing at them. Really, to look at us anyone would think we were a happy family, he thought, a trifle bitter and thankful at the same time.

It really was a happy family which, half an hour later, sat down to a breakfast of roast meat, while Indepentia lay crowing on a blanket, playing with her hands in the day's first sunlight.

"If *you* don't think it's so bad that they've gone, John, *I* don't think it's so bad, either," said Louise magnanimously.

"I thought they were horrid beasts," Cathie exclaimed.

"Don't show off," said Francis.

"You mind your own business," Cathie snapped back.

"Don't start rowing, or I'll throw you out!" John warned them sternly. But he had to laugh, for the row was a happy row, no one really meant anything by it, and it was such a nice reminder of life as it had been in the past. How often Father and Mother had had to intervene in quarrels!

"No arguing now!" he repeated with satisfaction, although it was no longer necessary at all. The children had become entirely engrossed in gnawing the meat from tough, stringy rabbits' legs.

CHAPTER 10

The Great Cloudburst

But it was not a happy family which, ten days or so later, experienced the first great cloudburst of the autumn at the foot of the Blue Mountains.

The rain poured down as pitilessly as it had that night in the wagon camp at Soda Springs, and this time the children had to endure the terrifying tempest without any shelter whatever.

Shaking and trembling, they sheltered in a ravine, against a moss-covered mountainside which was bare and greenish and slippery in less than no time. The rain poured down, and wild brooks and streams arose everywhere. Whole shrubs and trees were uprooted and carried away; great clods of earth and stones were torn loose; all the water-courses were suddenly full to the brim. The valley, encircled by a ring of menacing black mountains, was soon submerged; clumps of brushwood stood out like black islets above a sea which, lashed by the rain, rolled and splashed in gray waves.

The rain cut and scourged the little group of children cowering in the fissure, sticking to the side of the mountain. They stood with their faces turned to the rough rock wall, down which the rain gushed in a curtain of water. Breathing was difficult. The hard, icy jets of rain buffeted their backs; it was as if they had no clothes on their bodies. Stones and rocks were dislodged and sent rolling downward, forming a source of real danger.

John stood bent over Lizzy, who shuddered between his legs, screaming with terror, and over Indepentia—a soaked little bundle lying on the ground in a sopping wet bed of dense dwarf shrubs. He stood with the palms of his hands pressed to the mountain wall, and protected the two little ones with his back, shoulders, and head

as well as he could. A small, sharp stone had hit
the back of his head. The blood was washed away
immediately by the pouring rain.

"This can't possibly last long," he got out between clenched teeth, to Francis, who was leaning
against the cliff with his face in his upraised folded
arms.

Of all the children, Matilda had always been
least afraid of the forces of nature. But now even
her eyes were wide and black with horror in her
dripping face. Her short hair stuck to her head
like a smooth, dark helmet, and she had even
ceased to feel the water gushing down between
her grimy shirt and her little brown body.

She stood jammed between John and Francis.
Louise and Cathie were crouching huddled together under the cliff, with their hands on their
heads. Behind them, Anna lowed nervously without stopping. Oscar lay between her four legs. He
lay panting with open jaws, his tongue hanging
out as if he was thirsty.

The rain pelted down. It hurt, even though the
cold had partly numbed the children. "Hail," John
muttered. Hail and rain came down together. The
hail cut and slashed; their skin was beaten until it
bled, but the rain washed all the blood away.

"Stick it out!" John shouted over Francis's head to the terrified girls.

Pitiful, stifled crying sounded through the drenched fur of the little heap called Indepentia. John gritted his teeth so hard that they grated.

Distractedly he looked at the pile of sleeping bags with which he had covered the rifles and the powder horn. What on earth was proof against this deluge? A feeling of despair seized him. They were no longer so terribly far from their objective, only this last mountain chain, and then. . . . But without serviceable firearms, and without material for setting snares . . . ? What would become of them?

They were so paralyzed and breathless that they did not even notice that the rain was beginning to slacken off. Nevertheless, John suddenly became aware of something—another sound, another rushing noise, more irregular, creaking and cracking, ominous, a sound which swelled and grew.

The cleft in which they were standing had itself become the bed of a stream; they were up to their ankles in swiftly flowing water, but they only knew that because they could see it, on the rare occasions when they were not keeping their eyes tightly closed.

John now saw that the stream was beginning to rise; gray earth came along with it, stones, torn-off branches, fragments of roots. And when he looked farther up, toward where the pouring came from, he saw the top of a great tree come slowly sliding down. The branches scraped, cracking and creaking against the side of the mountain.

Slowly, slowly, the tree came forward. The water flowed, foaming and boiling under it. But it was possible that the tree would suddenly come loose—fifty yards or so above where the children were standing, the sides of the ravine parted more widely. Propelled by the water, the huge tree might develop such great speed there that the children would not be able to get clear in time. The way down was difficult. They could not descend very quickly; besides, it was treacherously slippery everywhere.

The other side of the ravine was less steep than that against which they were sheltering. It was their only chance.

"Francis!" John shouted. He pointed to the tree. "We've got to get up on the other side. You go in front. I'll come last."

Without a word, Francis took Lizzy's hand and jumped over the stones, through the running water, to the other side. John pushed Louise and Cathie forward, and gave Matilda a hard shove, sending her behind Lizzy.

"Go on, go on, climb up, keep behind Francis, hold on tight to the bushes!"

He himself seized Indepentia in his left arm, pushed the others onward with his right, and hoisted himself up behind them. John measured the distance; he measured the height and breadth of the monster tree, which was steadily sliding forward, filling the ravine with a terrifying cracking of rending boughs. The children were high enough now, he thought. They were safe.

The mass of branches came nearer and nearer to the place where the ravine widened. The guns and sleeping bags were still lying down below, and there stood Anna bellowing for help at the foot of the slope; she was standing with her forefeet on a boulder, and the water was spattering up round her legs. Oscar, who had run after the children, stood barking above John's head.

"Come on, take this!" John pushed Indepentia into Cathie's arms. "Hold her tight, mind!"

He slid down again into the path of the tree. Up to his knees in the steadily rising water, he seized the sleeping bags and threw them as far as he could up the slope, where they were caught by the brushwood. He grabbed the rifles, slung two over his shoulders, and let the third one lie. He picked up the powder horn and threw it upward; it landed close to Francis. He took Anna by the rein round her neck, and hauled her along. The poor beast climbed valiantly. John pulled as hard as he could, digging in his heels, and holding on tight to bushes.

The tree reached the opening and stuck there, instead of suddenly shooting through it. A projecting point of rock barred its way. The water foamed and seethed more and more violently.

"Look, it's stopped raining!" Cathie suddenly screamed.

John looked up. He had not noticed that the sky was clearing, so intense had been his absorption in the danger that had menaced them. And Anna was still not safe. That tree could start moving again at any minute.

Francis had walked down to collect the sleeping bags. The girls lay on their stomachs on a sort of little plateau, holding their arms out to take them from him. Only Matilda kept her eyes fixed on Anna, who was advancing slowly but surely.

"Come on, Anna, come on!" she kept calling.

The cow was high enough now, but she climbed stubbornly on, in order to get close to the children.

John was just on the point of going down again to rescue that precious third rifle when suddenly there came a noise as if lightning had struck somewhere. With rending violence the tree tore loose and slid down the ravine, sweeping in front of it everything that lay in its path. With an ear-splitting din of scraping, creaking, and crashing, it slid below the children, slid past them. Speechless, they watched it go.

The weather had cleared. The sun was even breaking through the clouds. It was a bright, still warm, autumn sun, which made the mountain slopes steam and smoke.

But the children were shivering. Their heavy clothes stuck to them like suits of armour. Their hair still dripped. There was nothing with which they could rub themselves dry. Trembling, the little girls cried. Cathie tried to be brave, but her chin twisted and shook.

"Keep moving!" John ordered them. "Don't stop moving. Climb up and down a bit. I'm going to have a look around."

When he came back an hour later, he found a wretched little bunch of children, huddled on top and under and beside each other. Only Francis was walking about, round and round his sisters, like a sheep dog round its sheep. But he was purple with cold.

John scattered the group. "Come on now, look alive—we're going a bit farther up. There's a slope up there which is right in the sun, out of the wind, and complete with a clothes horse for our things."

Like a brood of bedraggled chicks, they limped along behind John.

The spot he eventually indicated to them really was more favorably situated than they had dared to hope. It was sheltered and sunny; the tops of the low cranberry bushes were already dry. The slope was so steep that the comparatively low sun shone almost perpendicularly on it. Even the mist was warm there, warmer than their benumbed bodies.

John pointed proudly to an old dead tree, lying diagonally across a gigantic boulder. Its branches stuck up in the air, silver-gray from wind and weather.

"That's what we'll hang our clothes on," said John. By way of giving an example, he began to throw everything off. A few minutes later, the entire wash was hanging to dry.

Lizzy had quite forgotten all the misery, and was running around naked, squealing with delight. John was busy rubbing Indepentia, rubbing until her whole tiny body was a fiery red. He did not care at all now how much she screamed. She had to get warm.

On John's orders, Francis had cut thin branches from the bushes and shrubs, and had stripped the leaves off them; he gave one to each of the children. "Go on, beat each other! Beat each other!" he ordered them.

"The one who gets reddest gets a prize!" John called. Tough little devils, he thought proudly, looking at his brother and sisters as they ran about waving their branches.

Louise was the only one who did not join in; she stood a short distance to one side, beating her legs —the part of her which needed it least.

"Go on, Louise, or I'll come and do it for you!" John warned her.

With a shout, Francis leapt toward her, branch upraised. She fled like a doe. John laughed until he shook, kneeling on the ground, with Indepentia in his arms. He rocked her to and fro, and she stopped crying. He walked over to the dead tree, and reached up. His own shirt was dry already.

He wrapped the child in it. Then it was time to think of himself. He started rolling like a foal among the rough cranberry bushes; in less than a minute he was red as fire and covered with scratches. And warm.

The children's shirts were the first things to dry. They capered round in those dirty-white, shapeless garments. Cathie had won the prize. She glowed from top to toe, her ears burned, her toes tingled. She became quite still with ecstasy when John handed her a mug of milk from Anna. "Oooooh," was all she said.

The watertight tinderbox in John's belt really had remained dry inside. And the wood of the dead tree was dry enough now to use.

When a good fire was blazing, they remembered that they were hungry. But there was nothing to eat.

"My powder has got to get bone-dry first," said John.

They had spread the sleeping bags out in the sun. John shook the contents of the powder horn out onto one of them. He tore a strip off his shirt, and began to take the firearms to pieces and dry them. He frowned.

"I think I'd better set a few snares, to begin with," he said.

More and more items of clothing got dry. John was away setting snares a long time; and when he returned, they were all fully dressed. He was carrying something in his arms—a big wood pigeon —probably old and tough. "Killed by the hail," he said. There was just enough to give everyone a morsel of roast meat. John set a last snare and put the skeleton down beside it.

They sat together in the twilight, in the ruddy glow of the fire. They ate some of the hard, acid cranberries. Lizzy and Indepentia had had some milk. Heaven grant they might keep that power of recovery which Fort Boise had given them for some time longer, John thought to himself.

The sleeping bags were still damp, but they crept into them all the same, two by two, as close as possible to the fire. And they slept soundly through the howling of the wolves.

CHAPTER 11

The Bear's Den

That cloudburst had only been a foretaste of what was to come. The children tramped through a wild country of deep chasms and of treacherous clefts hidden under dense brushwood; of turbulent streams and of slopes which were so thickly overgrown as to be quite impossible to traverse here and there.

They pushed on farther and farther to the northwest, setting their course by the sun; they tramped across hills and through narrow defiles; they wandered around for hours, sometimes for days, before they could get any farther.

Showers of rain and hail and blinding snowstorms hammered them, demoralized them, broke them. It froze every night these days; their moccasins were worn out, they had wound strips of wolf's skin round their feet, but that was not enough. In the higher regions they waded through deep snow up to their knees, up to their hips. John carried Lizzy and Indepentia by turns.

The children were hungry.

The pistols and rifles had become unserviceable. After that first terrible downpour, John had not been able to get them right again; they had been left behind. All except the breechloader; that still worked, though not always—sometimes it misfired. But they had to use it sparingly anyway, for there was not much powder left.

John had shot a couple of wolves, and once he had killed a lean mountain goat. They set traps and snares, but they seldom caught anything. Sometimes they found only a skeleton next morning—in that case, some other hungry animal had come by a meal easily for once. They drank rain water and melted snow. Their feet froze and swelled up; open cuts and wounds came on them, which got dirty.

The cow grew thin; her ribs stuck out like sticks. Nevertheless, she still yielded a very little milk. She fed on tufts of grass—the children scraped the snow away for her where that was necessary; and she also ate moss.

They were only covering five or six miles a day now. John walked ahead with black-ringed, dispirited eyes. The children straggled along behind him, dull with despair, listless with exhaustion. They dragged themselves on, on their blistered, frozen feet.

The little ones wailed and cried a hundred times a day; at the slightest provocation they sat down and refused to go any farther, but John drove them mercilessly onward. Lizzy had long ceased to receive any of the precious milk. Indepentia looked half-starved. She was so weak that her crying was hardly audible, and John sometimes doubted whether she was still breathing.

The clothes they had been given at Fort Boise— it seemed years ago now—hung round them in tatters, crumpled and weather-stained. They hardly spoke to each other. The children were afraid of John, even more afraid than they had been that time in the Snake Valley, where they had suffered from thirst, heat, flies, and mosquitoes. He was now even harder, even stricter, even more inexorable than he had been then.

One evening they were sitting in front of a big fire.

Darkness fell early now; autumn was nearing its end. They stretched their purple, chapped, and swollen hands toward the warming glow. John sat morosely some distance from them, in utter wretchedness. Round about, wolves howled. Sometimes a pair of eyes would smolder out of the darkness.

The children dropped off to sleep. They had had nothing to eat. John remained awake, keeping guard. He had Indepentia in his arms, with a wolf's skin wrapped round her.

He forced himself to stay awake by thinking of old times. The memory of those times was his only refuge. He no longer dared to dream of the future. He hardly dared to hope that they would ever reach the Columbia Valley.

He thought of old times. With an effort, he tried to picture Sunday morning on the farm near St. Louis. It smelled nice in the house; Mother had been baking cakes. Lizzy was lying in the cradle;

she crowed and beat the air with her little hands. She had fat little arms. Indepentia's arms were like twigs.

He pined so terribly for those old times. For steaming maize mush, for cake, for a fire on a hearthstone, for hot milk, for the deep bass voice of his father, for his mother's warm hand on the back of his neck—she always stroked the hairs on his neck the wrong way. For fat baby arms—oh, for fat baby arms. Suppose Indepentia. . . .

He did not dare to follow his thought to the end. If she had to die, he would prefer that they all died. And all at the same time. Not one after the other. Dear God, not one after the other.

A very faint sigh came from Indepentia's tiny mouth; a little moan. He listened hungrily; he smiled in the darkness. He wrapped the wolf's fur close about her again. He rocked her in his arms. That kept one awake, too. He must not fall asleep. Wood had to be put on the fire. Those glowing wolves' eyes must not come any closer.

Next day Cathie stubbornly refused to go any farther. With gritted teeth, John seized her roughly by the arms, threw her across his knee, and spanked her until he could spank no more. Then he put the dazed child down on her feet again.

"Will you go on now?"

She nodded without speaking. She did not even cry. He would sooner have seen tears—then Cathie would have been more like herself. But she nodded dully, and began to walk.

He turned away with a jerk. He did not want to see the faces of the other children.

That same afternoon, Anna slipped and fell awkwardly on her side. Louise, who was walking next to her, was pinned beneath her. She shrieked. When the cow scrambled to her feet again, Louise could not get up. John saw that her right leg lay twisted under her in a strange fashion. He wanted to straighten it. She screamed.

"It's broken, John."

It *was* broken. Even a child could see that. He was completely at a loss as to what to do. He stood looking at Louise, with his hands hanging helplessly at his sides. Louise moaned, and twisted and turned her head and shoulders from the pain.

They could go no farther. They made a fire. The place where they happened to be was fairly suitable.

The leg began to swell. John climbed to a small snow field lying a short distance higher up the mountain, and there he made hard snowballs, which he threw down to Francis to catch. When there was a whole pile of them, John descended again. He pressed the snowballs against Louise's leg. He had once seen his father do that to the injured leg of a horse. The swelling had gone down then.

And that happened in this case, too. But it took a long time. Not that it mattered—they could not get any farther today, anyway. He did not dare think of the days that were to come.

They made their bivouac. When it was dark, Louise said to John, looking at him in the flickering light of the fire, with eyes big and black in her white, gaunt face, "You go to sleep, John. I'll call you if anything happens, and if wood has to be put on the fire. I can't sleep, anyway."

A minute later he was sleeping like a log.

It was Oscar who made the discovery next morning.

For a long time, he had been running round restlessly sniffing, nosing at a scent which he would not leave but did not really dare to follow either. Francis went along with him. "Not too far!" John called after them.

Oscar and Francis disappeared in the brown

brushwood. Suddenly loud barking rang out, and Francis came running back. He beckoned with his arm, and shouted, "John, John, your gun, quick!"

John ran. Francis went in front of him. They cleared a path for themselves between the swishing branches, to a place where Oscar's shrill barking was accompanied by a bloodcurdling growling.

In a hole half dug in the ground, sheltered by a low niche in the wall of rock and well hidden behind dense undergrowth, an enormous old bear lay half on its back, half on its side. It growled terrifyingly, with open jaws.

When the children appeared behind the dog, the bear tried to get up. It raised itself a little. With lightning speed Oscar leaped forward and fixed his teeth in its throat. The bear uttered a terrible roar, and rolled on to its feet with one last spasm of effort. Reeling, it stood on its shaggy, tufted hind legs.

John aimed, pulled the trigger—the gun misfired. But at the same moment the bear fell over on its back again, with Oscar on top of it.

John walked round a few paces, and tried to fire a second shot at its head. But the rifle misfired again.

The bear tried to get up once more. It could not.

With a mighty swing of its left forepaw it swiped Oscar away. The wolf dog yelped loudly, but sprang back to the animal at once, and set his teeth in its throat for the second time.

The boys stood by, breathless. John did not even try to fire a third shot. The bear could do no more; it had been old and dying when Oscar found it— a solitary old male; and now the dog was putting a quicker end to its life, that was all. The blood flowed away from the wounds on its neck. It did not last long.

It was impossible to get Oscar to leave the dead bear. The boys walked slowly back to the girls.

"A bear—dead in his lair," Francis got out.

The hollow faces showed a certain dull interest. Louise's only answer was a moan.

John sat down by the fire, and pointed to Francis's hunting knife. He wanted it. Francis gave it to him. John sharpened it against his own. When the two knives were as keen as razors, he went off again, back to the bear. Francis had to stay with the others and look after the fire.

John was busy all day. But when he had finished, the bear's hide had been scraped clean inside, and the girls sat with their legs buried in the old animal's thick winter coat. Big pieces of bear's meat were roasted above the fire; the fat dripped hissing into the flames; they could all eat as much as they wanted. John had set traps and snares, using the bear's flesh as bait. He wanted to catch wolves, for the sake of their furs.

"We'll stay here," John decided. "We'll move to the bear's den, it's big enough for all of us to lie in it. I'll cut the brushwood away from in front, so that we can have a fire. We'll be warm and sheltered there. We'll stay there until the bear's meat's gone, and we'll eat as much as we can every day. Higher up there's enough snow for water, and perhaps Louise will have less pain if she can lie down for a few days. I'll see to it that we get wolf skins, Francis will see to wood and to the fire; and the others can go out and look for food for Anna, from morning till night."

That was their only chance. The cow *had* to be kept on her feet. She had to be able to carry Louise on her back—otherwise, how would they ever be able to get on?

The bear's lair stank. A pungent, rancid odor stung their nostrils. But they had the feeling that they were moving into a house. A deliciously warm, safe house, with a roof and a floor and a fire in an open hearth. Cathie, who had eaten until she was round and satisfied, began to perk up again.

"Oooh, what a smell! But it's nice and warm!" She nestled down cosily against the wall.

"It'll soon be Christmas," said Francis suddenly.

"Don't say such idiotic things," Cathie suddenly burst out, with tears in her eyes. "How on earth can you talk about Christmas *here?*"

"At Christmas we shall be at Dr. Whitman's mission station," John said slowly. "Then we shall have goose with roasted apples, and cake and. . . ." They listened in amazement to this cheerful note from John's lips.

"And nuts and oranges," Cathie added, suddenly feeling that she wanted to hear about Christmas after all. "And pancakes with bramble jelly."

"And at Christmas, we'll dance," Matilda chimed in, in a dreamy tone, with her eyes fixed on the fire.

Or we shall be lying under the snow, thought John; but the children don't need to know that.

He listened thankfully to Francis and Cathie bickering. Was it to be red or black bramble jelly? Louise lay without speaking, but her eyes were open, and she was the only one who saw John smile. Suddenly she began to understand him a little.

They stayed in the bear's den for six days. By

then the meat was gone. And John dared not stay any longer. The mountain passes were already deep under snow.

Another six arduous days' marches followed. In three days they had climbed a mountain ridge. In two days they had descended it on the other side. Yesterday they had stood at the foot of the next ridge, and John had pointed to its snow-crowned top and said, "Perhaps this is the last." No one believed any longer that there was a last.

Now they were plodding on through the deep snow. It really looked as if they would never reach that ridge. John was crueler and harsher than ever; he was at his wit's end, and he constantly had to conceal his despair. Their only chance of salvation lay in his remaining mercilessly severe.

He walked on in front. He had to lift his feet as if heavy weights hung on them. He made a path for the others. Under the snow the rocky ground was sharp and rough, but even the snow pierced his sore swaddled feet as with a thousand needles. His heart thumped against his ribs. Indepentia, who weighed nothing, was a leaden burden in his aching arms.

Doggedly pushing on, he came nearer and nearer to the top. Once he was there, he would lay Indepentia down and go back and fetch the others. He could already hear them crying. Now and again he caught the voice of Francis from below, urging the girls on and talking to Anna. Louise was a brick. Ever since they had left the bear's den, she had not made a sound of complaint. Her broken leg dangled limply down Anna's lean flank.

He had reached the top. He made his last steps slowly.

That . . . that was impossible! How could it be, so—so suddenly? It was such a wonderful sight, what he saw there. So splendid, so unbelievable, so . . . it must be an optical illusion, he thought. He shook his head and shut his eyes. Then he opened them again. It was *not* an optical illusion, it was what he had been hungering for all these weeks, and now that it was there he could not believe it.

Far below him, far below this last chain of the Blue Mountains, lay a wide green valley, with trees and shrubs still clad in their autumn yellow. There were the small square shapes of a few log cabins, a thin plume of smoke rose from a chimney —it was the mission station of Dr. Marcus Whitman. It was Oregon! It must be the Columbia Valley! Down there he saw a winding, silver ribbon with edges of luxuriant green.

He did not look round at the others. He did not beckon and he did not wave; he did not shout. He stood motionless, gazing down, and he let them come.

CHAPTER 12

Oregon at Last!

Now their bleeding feet had climbed the last mountain ridge; now they were standing on the crest of the whole range, staring down into that broad green valley in the west. Behind them stretched a labyrinth of mountains cut by deep canyons, a hard, savage world in black and white. Like patient snails they had found their way, creeping up and creeping down, a tiny caravan of insignificant dwarfs in the land of the giants.

Beneath them, at the foot of the long last slope,

stretched the green valley, warm in its autumn colors.

Yonder in the depths wound the Columbia River.

Farther off, extending far into the remote distance, where the whole world turned blue, the majestic hill country of Oregon lay spread before them in a tremendous panorama. There was the land where all promises and dreams would come true!

The children stared down. They shivered. John did not allow them much time to rest. With groping steps, he began the long descent. Slowly they came behind him, down—down—down. Oscar ran on in front.

John walked as if in a dream. His legs, swathed in pieces of wolf's hide, seemed totally numb. Nevertheless, they continued to carry him. A strip of leather kept his long hair out of his eyes. On his back he was carrying little Lizzy, in his arms the bundle of fur containing Indepentia, who had not made a single movement, not given a sign of life, for many hours now, and perhaps was dead. . . .

Behind John waddled the cow. She groaned; descending was much more difficult for her than climbing, and her worn hoofs were split down to the quick.

On her skinny back, Louise and Matilda sagged like limp dolls, wrapped in rags and wolfskins. It was as if there was no light left in their eyes, no blood left in their cheeks, no strength, no sap, left in their whole bodies. Their hair hung long and tangled round their heads.

Francis and Cathie were walking, their faces gray, gaunt, and dull. Francis urged Cathie onward in a weak voice, which she did not hear.

They crept down the slope, they stumbled, fell, scrambled to their feet again, dragged themselves on, coughing, panting. Even now, John still had the greatest difficulty in keeping them moving—still, with the end in sight, they would sooner have lain down and died where they were; still he had to pause and wait, chivvy them, be rough and hard.

And at last, at last, in a silence that was more heart-rending than the loudest weeping, they stood in the valley before the door of Dr. Whitman's log house.

John pushed the door open with his knee.

A young woman with a pale, weary face, came forward.

John looked at her.

She uttered an unintelligible cry when she saw the group of little ghosts—the wasted children's faces, the cow which was no more than a caricature of a cow.

The children remained silent, they could not say a word. John made a feeble movement with his arms. Narcissa Whitman put out her hands and took the little bundle from him. She motioned to him to follow her.

Cathie tripped over the doorstep. She remained lying there until Francis helped her up. John helped Matilda to slide down from the cow, and set her on her feet. She tottered into the house. He helped Louise off too, but she fell moaning to the ground, and could not get up. He could not help her. He went inside.

They came into a big kitchen. There was an enormous brick stove in it, and the room smelt of savory meat cooking with salt.

A man was standing there. He was dressed like a trapper and wearing a woolen cap. His eyes stared incredulously out from under bristly eyebrows. He said not a word; his gaze traveled from one to the other, dwelt a second or two longer on John, and then turned to Narcissa, his wife.

She had laid the baby on the table; hastily she

tore open the fur and the rags. Their own only child, a little girl, had been drowned in the river two years ago. But when she saw what was lying under those rags stiff with dirt, she backed away. With wide, staring eyes, she looked at Indepentia. Dr. Whitman followed her gaze. A breathless silence hung in the kitchen.

John's suspense was unbearable. His eyes begged for an answer to his unspoken question.

"Perhaps there's still some life left in it," was all Marcus Whitman could say.

Narcissa Whitman took the tiny skeleton into the bedroom with her. Her husband started to take the other children to a washroom in one of the outbuildings of the mission post. But John refused. He jerked his head in the direction of the door through which Mrs. Whitman had disappeared.

"Lad, lad, you can't do anything to help there, anyway," said Dr. Whitman.

John still said not a word. He remained stubbornly standing where he was, looking at the door. But then he suddenly remembered. Louise! Louise is still lying outside!

He motioned to the Doctor. Whitman followed the strange boy out of the house. He lifted the girl, who lay unconscious on the ground, up in his arms. She did not weigh much more than that tiny baby should have weighed. Her leg was inflamed and swollen. Her head dangled limply back like a little bird's.

Dr. Whitman spread a blanket out on the floor in the kitchen and put her down on it. He poured drops of milk, one by one, between her half-open lips. When she came to, he laid another blanket over her, and let her lie there while he went back to the others.

John had vanished. As if drawn by a magnet, he had walked through the doorway through which Indepentia had been carried. He came into a sitting room with a table and chairs and a ticking grandfather clock, a mirror and books; another door stood open and, as if in a dream, he walked through into a bedroom.

Narcissa Whitman was bathing Indepentia in warm water. John stood behind them. He saw the tiny frame, nothing but sticks of bones and skin, being rubbed and massaged with warm oil, by gentle hands—he saw her being wrapped in clean woolen cloths. But still she gave not a single sign of life. Narcissa Whitman held a mirror in front of her mouth. Did the glass become misty or not?

She couldn't be sure; she rubbed the mirror clean on her sleeve, tried again, was still not sure.

Carefully, she pressed a few drops of warm milk and water between the baby's purple lips. John held his breath. He reeled on his feet.

At last, the tiny throat made a movement as if it was swallowing, and a sound came out of it, even fainter than the cheeping of a little bird.

When John heard that, he fell to the ground, threw his arms round Narcissa Whitman's knees, and burst out sobbing. His shoulders shook, his arms dropped to her feet, he collapsed on the floor and wept and laughed at the same time.

Mrs. Whitman let him cry it out. She stroked his hair, deeply moved.

Finally John got up. He did not look at her. Without saying a word he stumbled from the room.

Meanwhile, Dr. Whitman had been busy with the others. He had made them presentable and human again, washed them, cut their hair, and given them clothes. Now they were sitting at a table in the kitchen, gorging like wolves.

The whole night through, Narcissa Whitman sat up with the baby in her lap, concentrating all her strength on trying to keep her alive.

John, washed and tidied up, in clean clothes, was sleeping on a fur at her feet. Dr. Whitman was lying on a camp bed beside her. He lay with his hands folded behind his head, and with open eyes. He did not need to look at John to be constantly aware of the boy's presence. There was something about that lad, something emanated from him— a strength of will such as Marcus Whitman had never yet encountered.

Marcus Whitman smiled in the darkness. Before they went to bed, something had happened. He could still feel that shaking, thin body against his, that boy's head on his shoulder.

"Take the load off me," John had sobbed, "I can't go on, I can't. They don't love me any more, they couldn't understand, and I love *them* so much. I've beaten them, I've dragged them along . . . and now we've got here, and they don't love me any more! Please, won't you help me? I can't go on!"

Dr. Whitman had patted him on the back. He had spoken soothing words to him. But that had not been any use. John had repeated his question, urgently, imploringly, with burning eyes.

"Won't you take care of us? I want to . . . play

with them again." That last had been spoken very
softly. Like an admission of guilt.

It had moved Dr. Whitman more than anything
else. The boy had done something superhuman—
hardly any grown man could have done it. But he
had suffered much under his far too heavy task and
responsibility, and now he wanted to play again
. . . to play with his sisters and his brother and
the baby.

It was no trifle, to take seven children into his
household—seven more mouths to feed. Seven children, a wolf dog, and a cow!

If his wife had not been so wretched, then . . .
well, there was no telling what he might have
decided. But that solitary life there, with nothing
about her except, now and again, hypocritical
Indian faces, was killing her. And yet there *was*
a future in this country. Sometime, in the distant
future, farms and villages and perhaps even towns
would arise. And to achieve that, men and women
were needed who were made of the same stuff as
the Sager children.

He put out his hand and touched his wife's knee.

"I believe she'll make it," Narcissa whispered.
"She's breathing regularly now."

"It's a miracle," the doctor-missionary whispered back. "It's all a miracle!"

"Oh, Marcus," came his wife's gentle voice. "Oh, Marcus, do you think you could possibly let them all stay here?"

A soft laugh sounded in his throat. He said something which Narcissa did not hear; but then she felt his warm hand squeeze her knee, and that told her what she wanted to know.

The following morning, as they sat at breakfast in the big kitchen, Dr. Whitman told the children of his decision.

"From now on, this is your home. And John's relieved of his job of father. Look upon me as your father, and my wife as your mother. May your heroic journey be the beginning of a highly promising future as American citizens. God bless our covenant. Amen."

On the third Sunday after they arrived, Indepentia was christened. With a beaming face, John held her for baptism. Fifty or so Indian men, women, and children who had been converted to Christianity attended the simple service.

When John left the log cabin which did duty as a church, carrying the child in his arms, he looked up at once at the snow-crowned peaks of the Blue Mountains. Then he bent his face down over Indepentia and whispered, "Little bag of bones, how on earth did you get here? I can't for the life of me understand!"

BIBLIOGRAPHY

Cannon, Miles: *Waiilatpu*. Boise, Idaho, 1915.

Egan, Howard: *Pioneering in the West*. Salt Lake City, 1917.

Fuller, George W.: *A History of the Pacific Northwest*. New York, 1931.

Ghent, W. J.: *The Road to Oregon, a Chronicle of the Great Emigrant Trail*. London, 1929.

Hough, Emerson: *The Covered Wagon*. New York, 1929.

Parkman, Francis: *The Oregon Trail*. 1849.

Vestal, Stanley: *Kit Carson*. 1928.

Vestal, Stanley: *Mountain Men*. 1937.

Vestal, Stanley: *Jim Bridger*. 1946.

Journal of the Lewis and Clark Expedition.